I0689242

The Renegades of Genoa

By: S. K. Anthony

Dedication:

To my family and friends for your help.

Special thanks to the real versions of these characters, without whom this book would be as dull as a bag of wet hair.

Edited by Sangeeta Mehta, without whose help it may have never been done.

Published by MacTech Services, Inc.

Prologue

The ships sailed forth, their deep bows cutting through the gentle waves of the old Roman sea. Behind them spanned a great burning and destruction. Only one faithful flag still stood, recalling the glory of this once proud Nicaean port city. It was now a burning blotch on the map, nearly unrecognizable in its devastation.

In the lead ship stood a figure, looking into the west and feeling the wind caressing his face and carrying his fleet into deeper water. Around him slunk the crew of this ship. They were diseased, covered in blotches and ignorant of their plight for they were under his control. When they were alive as citizens, soldiers, warriors of old, they fought against him with all the ferocity and desperation possible. It was all for naught however. Nothing could stop his advance and the sudden disappearance of the Nicaean prince was only a temporary setback.

"Arger!" he yelled over the clamor of the waves. Immediately, a figure came rushing over to him.

"Ah, dear Arger," he said putting a hand around the elegantly robed shoulders. "You have been with me for so long and worked so hard. Is everything ready?"

"Yes Axio Talphon," said the man. "All ships are in working order and the fleet is moving out with the utmost speed. It was a fortunate thing that, in taking the city, we managed to… *persuade* so many skilled sailors to our cause."

As he said that, Axio Talphon looked back at the working crew and laughed at the Arger's choice of words. The crew were witless and completely dependent on his whims. They still possessed however, full knowledge of their previous crafts and their efficiency was redoubtable. It would not be long till they reached their destination and Talphon turned to look at the setting sun with a scowl.

"Arger!" he said again, " where was that ship going to that stole my prize?"

"They were heading to southern Gaul, an area now called the Frankish coast and a great trading city called Marseilles, which you might recall as ancient

Massilia."

Talphon laughed to himself despite the anger rising up within him.

"…and so it begins," he said. "These thieves have forced my hand and brought me upon them. None will be able to stand in my way and once I have my treasure back and have infected the whole of that wretched region, I can return and commence on using it to bring this eastern world under my control."

He looked back and yelled at his crew, who stopped their tasks and gazed upon the figure at the front of the ship.

"Behold!" he said, pointing to the sky. *"The fires of our future are already alit. Soon we will make this vision reality and the glory that comes with it shall be ours. Witness the dawning of a new ORDER that will consume the world!"*

The arms of Axio Talphon cradled a red sky. It was dyed in blood and foreshadowed the great horror he was preparing to unleash upon the continent before him.

"TO MARSEILLIES!" he yelled and the ship roared in exhilaration.

Contents

Chapter 1

The solid stone church rose magnificently upwards. Its sacred walls and stained glass glittered in the evening sun and highlighted the importance of this wedding day. The rows of devout guests chanted in a chorus of voices, their heads bent in a disjointed union of Latin prayer along with that of the priest leading the marriage ceremony. It was all so formal, so beautiful and so boring

Meliore peeked down the row and saw her immediate family following suit without the slightest bit of distraction. She couldn't stand it, everything had already dragged on for an endless stretch of time. The solitary main doors were wide open, trying vainly to coax in a non–existent breeze. The only thing that did come in was the smell of the banquet from outside. It was maddening.

"How on earth could anybody withstand this? I can hardly tell what is happening and I doubt if many people here can either!"

While Latin was still a fundamental part of all masses in mid–fifteenth century Genoa, it was not a commonly understood language. The only groups of people who couple speak it were the clergy and those with enough free time for study. Certainly none of Meliore's busy merchant family could discern more than a few words and in the seventeen years of her life, she learned practically none at all.

This was an important wedding, though. It was the marriage of her best friend and cousin, Corbella, to a wealthy and powerful Venetian prince. It was hoped that the marriage would quell the simmering rivalry between the trading families that had sprung up as a result of the increase in demand for goods from the Byzantine and Turkish states.

All of these facts were meaningless to Meliore, however. In just over a week's time, a second convoy of royalty from Venice was due to land and the following day was to be her marriage to a second Venetian prince. Just as rapidly as her cousin's marriage was agreed upon, so too was Meliore traded off for the peace and prosperity of Genoa. And to a royal figure she had no idea existed merely a month ago!

Those pigs didn't even send a painting, the only thing I requested…. I wonder what he looks like?

Meliore's nervous daydream was interrupted by shuffling as the entire congregation finished their prayer and stood to their feet. Caught off guard, she blurted out before jumping up and feeling something crash against the top of her head.

"Oww, what for the...?" she said, turning around and seeing her uncle slumping back against the seat behind her. A hand clawed and gripped her shoulder, spinning her around into the livid face of her mother.

"Foolish girl, why weren't you saying your prayers and paying attention?" hissed her voice. "This ceremony has nearly concluded so pay attention!"

Meliore grimaced under the power of her mother's hand and focused back upon the wedding ceremony. Up on the dais, her cousin Corbella stood wreathed in a soft white dress with a heavy veil over her face, occasionally twitching in an uncomfortable looking way. A few feet away stood the prince. He was a corpulent fellow, wearing fine clothes and as immaculately groomed as a queen. This lavish care was pointless in her opinion, however. His face was greasy and pimpled, and he snorted every now and then as if the difficulty of breathing required him to clear his nose repeatedly.

Poor Corbella...

At last, the ceremony was over. The congregation arose and the prince moved forward to unveil the bride and seal the marriage with a kiss. Meliore felt the tension rising within her as he drew closer to Corbella, reaching under the veil and lifting it with eyes shut and lips puckered. Though Meliore couldn't see her cousin's face, she thought she could sense her struggle to get away. The audacity of this action made the priest pale, but it was no use. Only after the prince placed his kiss did he open his eyes.

Never before had Meliore seen such a look of shock and horror hit a man as quickly as it did to that prince. He reached with a thick arm and tore the headdress off the bride to reveal a young man, his face red and dazed, with a rope holding a wad of cloth in his mouth. Some of the children cried in laughter while the adults stood agape. The prince wheeled about as if he was looking for somewhere to run before seizing the fake bride and throwing him into the aisle. Immediately, the church exploded into yelling as the Venetians began accusing Corbella's family and the rest of the Genoas of treachery and humiliation.

As Meliore looked around, watching the rising anger begin to boil over, a glint of sunlight suddenly caught her eye. It was Corbella, hiding just outside the church, a polished mirror in her hand. She quickly waved Meliore over and disappeared again.

What in Peter's name? Meliore wondered as she crawled through the undulating mass of relatives crowding towards the center aisle of the church. Nobody was paying attention to her. A few of the men had started brandishing their fists and it was likely that the church would erupt in a fight. Despite the threat of getting trampled, Meliore was able to sneak through unnoticed.

The sound of the conflict died down by the time Meliore emerged into the open air. Pavilions and tents covered the ground, a silent encampment disturbed by a few people walking around and tending to the feast that was set to follow the wedding. It all flittered by: the cabbage and fish, the rose puddings and the freshly brewed bride ale.

That pudding smells delicious, she thought. What a waste. And what is Corbella doing?

Meliore stopped at the edge of the church grounds and looked around. The sun was just beginning to sink from its apex in the sky and a warm breeze was sweeping from the south across the city as the nearby mountains glowed in the brilliance of the spring day.

Again, a flash of light caught Meliore's eye and she saw her cousin in the shadow of a tree at the edge of a grove of woods. It took less than a minute for her to cover the ground at a full run. Behind her she could hear the commotion from the church beginning to spill over into the yard and the echo of faint crashes.

"Have a look at yourself!" cried Meliore as she drew next to Corbella. "You're a mess and have you any idea what you've done?!"

"Cut your tongue a second," said Corbella glancing around nervously. "I'm not a clod, of course I know what happened. We need to get out of here so follow me quickly."

Corbella led the way towards the mountains adjacent to their family houses. They ascended a long path surrounded by trees and came up to the livery barn. Meliore looked around nervously for the workers, but nothing stirred except for the occasional clattering as the horses kicked the walls.

At last, they drew up to their horses' stalls and hunkered down against the wall. They both stood and caught their breath for a moment. Both of their horses poked their heads out curiously. Stocatta was Meliore's, a moderate sized grey and he played with her hair as she sat. Mercurie snorted at Corbella a moment or two and nudged her before poking his head back into his stall.

"What was it like in the church when that ugly fellow kissed him?" Corbella asked, getting up and looking into the stall.

Meliore laughed and scratched under her horse's forelock. Despite the repercussions they would be facing, she cheerfully recalled the moment.

"I can hardly describe what my eyes saw. That prince was so shocked that if he was armed, he probably would have killed that guy who was masquerading as you. I can imagine the church yard at present actually. Everyone is out in the reception area, occasional fighting and lots of yelling. The servants probably don't even know what happened and nobody has realized that I'm missing yet,"

"So," she finally said looking up into Corbella's eyes. "…what DID happen?"

Corbella sighed and rested her head on the stall wall.

"Okay, I know it's against custom, but I simply had to see this prince I was supposed to spend the rest of my life with. Rich, powerful and everything is one thing, appearance is another. So I snuck over to his area and caught a glimpse of him."

Meliore laughed and slapped her cousin across the back of the calves.

"So you saw that ugly fellow? I was wondering throughout the ceremony what was going through your mind."

"There was ne'er a chance I was going to marry him after that. I happened to catch him while he was changing and….that was a sight that would have sent the fishermen for their hooks."

"Oh really now, he's not that bad!" said Meliore, trying to rein in her laughter a little. "He looked like a great happy guy with a laugh like…"

"…like a bowl of pudding," finished Corbella. "So I drugged one of his servants with that revolting wine my father hides in his room, dressed him up and left him helpless in my dressing room. I hid just in time to hear my father pounding on the door. He must have thought I was stalling because he dragged the poor fellow away without delay. He was in a great uproar about everyone waiting and how it was dishonorable for our guests to have been waiting this long."

They laughed a little while longer. The sheer audacity and success of it made Meliore laugh until her cheeks ached. At present, however, she caught her breath and returned to her senses.

"What now?" she asked. "Your father is going to kill you. I'm in enough trouble as it is. They will probably assume that I knew about it and helped you out."

"I told you that you hung around me too much for your own good, cousin…" Corbella said with a fading smile. "…and I don't intend on returning home…."

The last statement caught Meliore by surprise.

"Wha…you're what?"

"I'm not going home. I'm done; I refuse to live under Father's thumb anymore. I don't want to live a life like my mother did, or the life of a princess 'mongst the Venetians with that ugly tree knot."

"For Peter's sake, you are a dunce. What are you going to do 'stead?"

"Ah cousin, you don't do me enough credit. I managed to take plenty money to last awhile, but who can tell? I imagined we would figure it out on the go."

"We?"

Meliore stared at Corbella, not realizing what just happened at first. Her cousin was staring at her horse, refusing to make eye contact. A sudden pained expression took over her face and it seemed for a moment as though she was holding her breath.

"You want me to run away too?"

Corbella nodded, still stubbornly looking off.

"Oh dear…..not a chance," said Meliore. She recoiled a little and shook her head as a knot began tightening in her stomach. She knew from countless experiences that Corbella was incredibly persuasive and any argument was an uphill fight for her. But this was completely ludicrous, she had to make her see reason.

"Why not?" asked Corbella. "What is there for you back at home cousin and who is to say that we'll ever return? It's a wide world out there and we will find out place in it. It's certainly not here at home or married off to these princes."

"Come to your senses cousin! What are we going to do all on our own? We're girls! Never have we so much as set a foot outside the family houses without someone to watch over us, and now we're just going alone? My brother always scared me with stories about thieves and murderers down by the docks."

"Don't believe him, you know he always had it out for us. Remember when we were riding and his friends would spook our horses?"

Meliorie grimaced and nodded.

"All those times when Stocatta would buck and spin. I thought I would perish. But that is beside the point! Even so, the thought of going into town alone is frightening…"

" So what? Now's time to set out on our own. Don't tell me you always want to live as a wife or house maiden, never doing anything and occasionally harassed by her brother's idiotic jests."

"No, it's not a question. I everything is already decided. I am supposed to be married next week and you know that! My life is laid out for me."

At this, Corbella let out a laugh. It agitate Meliorie and she felt the panic within her double.

"Stop laughing, this isn't amusing!"

"Do you know who you're marrying, cousin?" Corbella asked. She cast Meliore a sidelong glance that did not bode well.

Meliore opened her mouth to respond, but Corbella cut her off before she could so much as take a breath to reply.

"You're marrying my fair prince's brother…" she said in a heavily exaggerated tone.

Meliore did not know what look her face took, but she could see what effect it had on Corbella, who laughed madly all over again.

"You're jesting," Meliore asked. "You cannot be certain of that?"

"Ah…. my dear cousin, do you think Venice is littered with princes? You're marrying that ugly bowl of pudding's brother. I can also guess that they'll take special precautions to make sure that you don't escape after the ordeal I caused."

"But, what if he's good looking?" asked Meliore.

"Are you willing to take the chance? Apples from a tree don't fall far from one another."

Meliorie sat back and closed her eyes. It was all too much and, as she feared, Corbella had many persuasive points. Was it all enough to warrant running away? She would already be in serious trouble because her deep connection with her cousin would certainly lead everyone to believe she had a part in the entire ordeal. Didn't she want to get married and live the life of luxury that her mother did? The door was open to that life, she just merely had to take it and step through it with her unknown husband and wealth, the security she always wanted, and prestige would be hers.

No, it was impossible to accept. She realized that she had been the product of her parents' expectations without any choice to the contrary as long as she was under their control. She simply never knew any other way. What else was the daughter of a wealthy merchant supposed to do except to get married in such a way as to expand and secure the business? It was her only purpose. A life intended to forge alliances through marriage. It was what her mother and cousins did. It was common, it was…sickening.

How many nights did she spend gazing across the bay, wishing for some act of providence to take her away from this life? Was this it? Was the reckless and ill–mannered cousin she grew up with just that instrument with which the heavens reached down and offered her a last chance to escape?

"Are you with me?" asked Corbella. Her face was lined in uncertainty and perhaps a little fright. If Meliore said no she would doom her cousin—her best friend—to face either her family's fury or the uncertainty of the world out there alone.

"Well?" Corbella asked again in a wavering voice.

"Not willingly, but someone has to keep an eye on you," said Meliore, brushing off Stocatta and standing up.

Corbella let out a shriek of joy and threw her arms around her cousin.

"You don't think I can make it alone?" she said, beaming and slackening her grip.

"You have not a chance, but with both of us at least we can suffer together. Now let's go. Do you have any idea where we can stay the night?"

"I have enough money to put us up at a place on the far side of town for a week or two. After that….well, we'll figure it out by then. Also, you might want to change into these," Corbella said, pulling out some clothes from her bag.

"These are men's clothes!" protested Meliore. "Look at this hat; it'll mess up my hair!"

Corbella threw her cousin a pained expression.

"We're girls and this is a dangerous man's world. If we don't want to be taken advantage of, I daresay we can't wander the streets looking the way we do. If we dress up as men, we'll be left alone at least."

Meliore held up her clothes and slowly nodded before looking outside the barn and into the western sky. Shadows stretched, overtaking the land in steadily increasing darkness, and a strong wind started to pick up off the ocean. She could feel the vibrant wind wrap about her as through it approved of the direction she decided to take her life. In just a month's time, who knows where they would be. Like the wind, wild and constantly uncertain of its course? Everything had rapidly fluttered in a new direction. The life she grew up knowing was gone in one simple moment.

"A little faster if you please," said Corbella, unlocking Mercurie's stall door and stepping in with her clothes. "I want to change quickly and find a place to stay. It's a long way off and I haven't had a bite since breakfast."

Meliore went into Stocatta's stall and started changing as well.

"What about our horses?" she asked.

"You cannot honestly expect us to take them along…," came a muffled voice. "Whatever shall we do with them? I have enough money for us alone and these two are will surely get us noticed."

Fully dressed, Meliore emerged out of the stall and looked as Corbella came out.

"I suppose this'll work," Corbella said, looking in a mirror she pulled out. "It is nearly nightfall. Ready?"

"One second," Meliore said rushing back into Stocatta's stall and wrapping her arms around his neck. He stepped back and craned his head around her. She could feel his nose checking for some kind of treat and she couldn't help but laugh despite the sadness she was feeling. They stood there for a while, she didn't know what to say to her longtime friend and wished she didn't have to leave him.

"I'll find a way to come see you…," she said, letting him lick her hand as she stepped away. She saw Corbella doing the same and waited till she said her goodbyes and came out of the stall.

"Let's go," said Corbella, wiping her eyes and turning down the aisle.

Chapter 2

It was the beginning of May in Genoa. The southeastern wind ushered in warm, humid air from across the Mediterranean and prepared the residents for the arrival of summer and with it, the hottest and driest time of the year. The increasing heat was only partially helped by the fact that the nights were comfortable and the wind never seemed to cease.

Corbella woke up, reluctantly at first with the morning sun in her face and the room's bare decorations strewn carelessly over the floor. In the corner, curled up and still happily sleeping, was Meliore on top of a pile of blankets.

She shuddered as her mother's scolding voice ran through her head. It was difficult getting any notion of her former responsibilities out of her mind. Since she ditched her wedding, Corbella found it hard to believe that, as long as she had money, she didn't have to do anything. The tavern owners came and cleaned up occasionally, food was provided for and most of all, there wasn't anyone brooding over you.

It has only been a day, right? No, it was the night before yesterday when we first arrived here. Did we really just stay inside all day and play around, trying to talk and act like men so we could start going outside in disguise?

She found herself thinking of their future and beginning to worry a little. Although necessities were a lot less expensive than she ever imagined and the money she had with her looked as though it would last awhile longer, it would run out at some point.

What are the odds that I can steal back home and get a little more money?

Corbella laughed at the thought. She was sure that it could be easily done. If anyone caught her, however, she'd be done for.

Ne'er a chance in hell am I going to go back. What's wrong with me, I'm beginning to sound like Meliore with this worrying.

She turned and looked over to her cousin, curled up in a ridiculous position but all together comfortable. Meliore was a great friend and gifted at a lot of things, but it wasn't likely she could sneak back into her house without getting noticed. Her house was smaller and her larger family made it slightly more crowded, especially now. Visiting relatives who came expectantly for her wedding were now probably being pacified as well as possible with leftover food and drink.

There's no going back for either of us. I suppose we could always become nuns…

Corbella laughed for a moment and rolled to the floor slowly. The covers slipped away and hung loosely off the bed. A nearby window rattled intermittently and when she threw the latch and opened it, a gust of wind blew through the room. The air was just a little warmer than comfortable and was perfumed by the ocean pounding the coast. It was peaceful bliss such as Corbella had never known before and she took this quiet moment to let it soak in.

"Why…?" trailed off a sleepy voice behind her after a moment.

Corbella turned around to find Meliore struggling and thrashing around.

"Why am I on the floor underneath all this?" she asked. She had a habit of shifting in her sleep and waking up halfway off the bed, stuck sideways, or jammed in the corner.

Meliore got up, dragging the covers off the floor and flopped back into bed.

"Corbella, what shall we doing today?"

"You actually want to do something? This is the life, lounging around like this is fantastic. I've scarcely wanted to do a thing."

The wooden bed squeaked as Meliore sat up, staring out the window with a frown on her face.

"I haven't a clue, it's vexing what we could do. It's just that I haven't taken to lying around as comfortably as you have."

"It's not like there is too much we can do anyways," Corbella said. "We've lived here almost our whole lives and a lot of people know of us. If our families—or worse the Venetians—stumbled upon us, we'd be in a lot of trouble."

"Ah me," she said, throwing herself back down. "It's just hard trying not to feel restless. I used to have to do so much at home and now, there's nothing at all."

"I know what you mean," said Corbella with a grin. "Just stick with it. Sloth does take some tough work getting used to."

She got up and lazily looked around. Meliore continued lying in bed with her head resting on her hands, rocking from side to side and humming to herself. It was half amusing, half annoying. Corbella knew that Meliore was so abstinently easygoing that it would be useless to rely on her for long–term plans without some generous prodding. It was not comforting knowing that it was up to Corbella to determine what they were going to do for the rest of their lives now that they were cut off from their families.

"Wait, where are you going?" asked Meliore as Corbella started getting dressed.

"No idea, I just wanted to put some clothes on. Did you want to go out now?"

"Of course. Let's go and get an early start!" Meliore said, springing up and digging through her pile of men's clothing.

"Are you kidding me?" asked Corbella with a laugh. "It's sure to be past midday now. There isn't another soul here who would consider this an early day."

"Whatever time it is works for me."

The docks of Genoa were spread out across one side of the harbor and lined with walls, towers and dockyards. Some of the ships coming in from the Mediterranean were for fishing but the bulk of Genoa's harbor traffic was devoted to its merchant fleet. It was this that propelled this semi–obscure fishing village into the forefront of the mercantile world. The fleets of trading ships brought startling wealth into these people's hands, making the chief business families some of the wealthiest in the entire region. It had also borne its share of rivalries, most chiefly with the other great trading center of Venice.

Corbella knew it was this rivalry that her marriage was supposed to subdue. The united cities would be well positioned to dominate every major facet of trade. It was going to be a glorious rebirth of the old Roman Empire, ruled by merchants and businessmen instead of soldiers and emperors. It I was all this that Corbella's mother told her the night before her wedding.

Perhaps she could see my doubt…

It didn't matter. Whatever was going on between the families was behind her now. She did not appreciate the ease with which they all were ready to marry off Meliore and her simply for a bigger part of the trading world.

Corbella looked across the waterfront for a while, seeing the ships of Venice at the far end of the harbor. It was strange that they appeared to be making no preparations to leave. The ships bobbed in the gentle swell with all her sails down and men at work on their decks. Usually, if they were preparing to depart, there would be a great continuous rush as the ships were loaded with supplies necessary for the trip. But from the looks of it, everything was quiet.

She heard the sound of running feet and turned to see Meliore jogging over.

"Took long enough," she said. "I was thinking of beginning this party without you."

"What party?" Meliore said, squinting and catching her breath. "The only one I was ever invited to was your wedding, and I didn't even get to the party part of that!"

Corbella laughed.

"I guess I can hardly fault you for that. Let's go and pick up your legs when you run. You look like a girl."

"Wait, I need to fix your hair," Meliore said, moving behind Corbella. "It looks like you have branches sticking out from under your hat."

"Hurry and don't let anyone see you. A fine pair of boys we are with you running like that and my hair sticking out."

"I realize that. Now if you would stop with your squirming, I'd be finished quicker!"

Corbella knew and Meliore quickly agreed the previous night that it was necessary to keep themselves constantly disguised as boys when they went out in public. It wasn't nearly as hard as they thought and compared to the long restricting dresses, pointy shoes, bodices and tight braids they normally had to wear as girls, it was much more comfortable. With the right clothes, they blended in relatively easily with the rest of the youths as long as they minded their voices and how they walked. After spending awhile perfecting their walks and voices, they felt everything was excellent except for one minor thing: neither could part with their hair.

"Are you finished yet?" Corbella asked, feeling a pinch as Meliore made swift motion. "*DID YOU YANK THAT OUT?*"

"Quiet! Some fellows over there are looking at us strangely. I'm almost finished, have you any idea how hard it is trying to make it look like you don't have sticks coming from under your hat?"

Once they were finished, they walked along the road leading through the dockside shops and lazily browsed around. Almost none of it was of any interest. Since they didn't have to cook, none of the great stores of exotic ingredients and spices were terribly appealing. The only things that were vaguely intriguing were the small array of trinkets from other Mediterranean cities. They had nearly finished perusing the shops and were just about ready to head back when a man waving his hands caught Corbella's attention.

Dirt from the surrounding street seemed to congregate around his stand and hardly anybody seemed to walk by it to disperse the mess. Even the sunlight itself didn't want to shine on the spot and his wares where hidden in the shadows. Corbella was interested in this man's obscure presentation and walked closer. The table was adorned with many little vials, icons and statues. The man who waved them over stood at an angle and his knuckles cracked as he waved a hand over the table.

"You two look bored with all the regular merchandise this place has to offer," came his voice. His mouth seemed to be stuck open and the words leaked out of it like air being forced through a broken horn. "I know the looks on your faces and it is my specialty to offer items you're not likely to easily find amongst the normal rabble."

Corbella could not help but be intrigued by this man's words and walked forward to see his collection. Meliore already was entranced by the statues and was looking at a scarlet one with a long beard and strange complexion. Corbella found herself mesmerized by the vials on the right side of the table. They seemed to glow faintly and ripple in unison as if they were subjected to some unseen tide. She stretched forward, close to a dark one with shadowy shapes moving around in it.

"What is that in there?" she asked, looking up to the shopkeeper.

The man let out a guttural jerking noise, something that could hardly be called laughing, and bent over.

"There's nothing alive in there, just the liquid."

"And the liquid is moving?"

"Yes. The onyx liquid is a favorite of mine from the far reaches of the east. It can make you forget something that just happened, or sometimes it makes you forget what you do next."

Corbella raised an eyebrow and looked hard at the man.

"Undoubtedly," she said sarcastically.

"It's not my job to convince you of what my wares are capable of. I know what they can do, or else I wouldn't bother with the effort."

At this point, the man put both hands on the table and looked squarely into her eyes.

"If I was lying, then surely you'd remember and come to find me. One cannot hide forever in the same city. Sooner or later, someone recognizes you."

He turned away from Corbella and looked at Meliore, who was playing with one of the statues.

"I like this one. What is it?" she asked.

As the two of them talked about it, Corbella gazed again into the vials. The man had thoroughly creeped her out. It was bad enough sounding the way he did, but what he said just now had really bothered her. She wasn't sure how, but it felt like he knew about their situation and was warning her. Stretching up and looking around, she found it hard to shake the feeling that everyone around her was suddenly aware of who they were.

Genoa's really not big enough to hide in forever. One day we will get caught if we stick around here.

"I'll take it!" said Meliore, putting the statue in her pocket and handing over some coins to the man.

He smiled toothily at her and nodded his head before turning back upon Corbella.

"And what about you, care for anything?"

"C'mon," said Meliore. "Get something, this stuff is surprisingly cheap!"

"Here," he said, reaching for faintly green liquid and putting it in Corbella's hand. "You'll need this someday when you need to not be yourself."

"So foreboding aren't we? Does this liquid make me crazed? Why would I need something that does that?" asked Corbella puzzled.

"Oh, not at all like that. It will be very handy though," said the man. "You can't predict all the needs and wants of your future like a story you've already heard the end to, but I do know this is going to help."

Corbella stared hard at the man before picking up the vial and looking into it. Just like the other liquids, it rippled and shone in her hand. Faint outlines, like green wisps of smoke swirled around the inside. At the very least, it was pretty and slightly mesmerizing so she shrugged and handed the man a few coins before turning to Meliore.

"Care for anything else?" she asked.

Meliore just shook her head and walked down the street.

"Let's see what there is to eat this evening."

"I know not what there is to do," Corbella said, pocketing the vial and slapping her pockets to make sure she still had all her coins. "There's nothing around here except for some vendors to eat at and walk around, and the food looks all the same. Everything has cabbage in it and I hate the stuff."

It was at this point that she turned her head and noticed someone walking besides them. He was older with a gray tinted beard and wearing the fine clothes of a merchant. At first sight, she panicked thinking that it was someone who recognized them and she made a twitch as if to run off. She stumbled instead and caught a second glance. He wasn't anyone she recognized and he came forward with a hand up, indicating to them to wait.

"Hello gents," he said softly. "Pardon my eavesdropping, but I can't help but overhear that boredom is gnawing at you both?"

Corbella held herself back and listened as the stranger talked in brief about who he was and what business he had interrupting them.

"I have a friend," he continued, "Gennaro's his name, who runs a part of the market here and also when chance favors it hosts a get–together for more prosperous people like us. Work is tough enough here without something to look forward to and there usually is this tolerable home–brewed ale that he brings out. Tonight however he has a couple of barrels of fine stuff from the church and that'll bring all manners of people to his establishment. Well to do youths like yourselves are welcomed to join us."

Meliore momentarily looked at Corbella. It was impossible to tell what she was thinking, but her slightly agape mouth made Corbella snicker.

"It seems as though you gents will be having some new guests," Corbella said. "We accept your invitation. Tell us what we need to know."

"Wonderful," said the man, clapping his hands together. "It is certainly the most delightful of things to have newcomers to join the merriment. After sunset, walk up the street from the fishermen's section of that market," he said, pointing across the harbor to another of the dockside markets. "Go up until you see a squat stone house on the left and a tall two story inn on the right. Turn on that street and go west for five houses and you'll see his name on the building. It'll be dark except for one lamp inside the window."

Corbella nodded slowly, going over the instructions in her mind. It didn't sound hard; she thought she knew exactly where the man was talking about.

"Who else is coming?" asked Meliore suddenly. "Are all of the merchants here invited?"

The man shook his head with a grimace.

"Not all of them are invited. There mainly are a lot of guests from other cities and Gennaro hosts them especially to help bolster his status. However, that whole incident at the church between the Venetians and those two trading families has gotten a lot of them people up in arms. None of them were told about tonight lest a war break out over a game of chance."

Corbella breathed a sigh of relief. This sounded exactly like the kind of event they were looking for and it would be terrible if either of her or Meliore's families were there to ruin it. Her reaction must have been obvious because the man looked from one to the other with vague interest.

"Have bad dealings with those families, or the Venetians?"

"You can say that," Meliore said after a quick laugh. "I never felt comfortable around them and with all these goings on…"

"Say no more," said the man, picking up his hands and cutting her off. "All I ask is that you don't bring whatever problems you might have with you tonight."

"Certainly not," Corbella said.

"The name's Giacamo," he said, turning and walking off. "Just in case you need it to help you get in."

They watched him walk off into a nearby building before starting off to their room. There was still plenty of time to get ready, but Corbella was eager for that night's adventure to begin.

"What do you think, can we trust him?" asked Meliore.

"I hardly think we can trust anyone and certainly nobody with our true story. Of course I still want to go, it's not like there's anything better to do. It's time for something exciting and as long as we keep our wits about ourselves we should be just fine. It might even be fun!"

"I suppose that is true. You can't be trusted alone so I have no choice other than to go with you."

"The usual weight on my plans," said Corbella, giving Meliore a whack on the shoulder. "I haven't led us that badly, have I? Have faith and let's go figure out what to wear and you need to give back that cloak. I don't remember lending it to you and you've been wearing it the whole day thus far."

Meliore shook her head, prompting Corbella to argue some more about stolen clothes. As they walked off, the sounds of the nearby waves crashing upon the shoreline drowned out their arguments. A fresh breeze came off the ocean, cleaning away the stale and stagnant air that had congregated in Genoa that afternoon. With it came a renewed feeling in the city. Lovely and pleasant for now, it foreshadowed something new and threatening. It had the potential to bring in a storm that would damage many of the buildings and drown more than a handful of sailors. Such was life; it was both invigorating and upsetting at the same time.

Chapter 3

"CORLIEU!" came a voice very close by.

"CORLIEU! WAKE UP!"

The abruptness with which he was shaken from his sleep and the light that pierced his eyes stunned Corlieu. He had never experienced anything like this before and he could feel involuntary lurches of dizziness voraciously pound his head.

"It can't be time to wake up, can it?" he said, trying to prop himself up and only succeeding in squirming around irritably. "I don't feel normal, what's going on? Why did you wake me up early?"

"Be quiet and listen," said a man, who hurriedly walked to a corner of a room and scooped up an armful of things, throwing them at Corlieu's feet. "We need to get you out of here. They're coming to burn this place down."

"Who is?" asked Corlieu, finally managing to sit up and noticing that he wasn't in his usual encasement.

"Later," said the man, rushing over and cramming some leather–wrapped papers and an odd assortment of things around a bewildered Corlieu, who was looking around and trying to figure out where he was.

"Am I… is this a boat?"

"No more questions!" said the man. "Here, you won't want to forget these," he said, holding out a pouch with a wink.

Corlieu reached out, missing twice before the man grabbed his hand and stuffed them in. Corlieu opened the bag and looked in, but his vision was cloudy and he couldn't tell what was in there. Closing the bag, he gave it quick shake. It made a soft jangle, similar to the clatter of pebbles but with a metallic tint.

"Thanks for keeping these safe," he said, tucking them away and unable to suppress a big smile.

A sudden cracking sound caught his attention. Part of the roof splintered and many steams of orange poured in from overhead. The wall splintered and a billow of black smoke puffed into the room. A cloud of it blasted Corlieu in the face and he felt the heat sear his eyebrows. Coughing, the man at Corlieu's side gasped and climbed into the boat, almost stepping on Corlieu who was flailing at his face.

"Hold on!" the man said.

Corlieu looked around bewildered and found nothing. The sides of his bed were smooth and offered no possibility of a firm grip.

"Hold onto what?"

The man shrugged and reached behind his back and gave a quick tug.

Corlieu was suddenly thrown forwards. He braced himself, lying flat on his back and watching as the man and he were launched through a rough tunnel. He was buffeted around mercilessly and there was one point where it felt like they were going to tip over. The man, sitting on his feet, leaned over and used a stick to push them back over however.

"WHAT FOR THE EMPEROR'S NAME IS GOING ON?" shouted Corlieu, nearly biting his tongue as they made a small drop and feeling his teeth clatter.

"I DON'T KNOW WHAT THEY ARE EXACTLY," yelled the man as he maneuvered the boat around a bend. *"WE HAD TO MOVE YOU ONCE ALREADY, BUT WAIT. I'LL TELL MORE IN A MOMENT!"*

Corlieu found himself buffeted from side to side and laid down putting his arms behind his head. They were going even faster and the bouncing was starting to really hurt his head.

Great… what kind of a world am I getting into?

"HERE WE GO!" the man yelled raising up his hands and squirming even harder against Corlieu.

Before he could ask, a brilliant light struck Corlieu and he squeezed his eyes shut. There was a temporary feeling of weightlessness where the only sounds were the yells of the man with him, then a sudden jarring splash. A torrent of water gushed into his face and he sat up, coughing and clearing his nose. The boat was half sunken and heading down a steady stream. Drawing off in the distance, Corlieu could just make out a flickering orange glow atop a hill surrounded in clouds.

"Where are we going?" asked Corlieu after a few moments of rubbing his eyes and trying to get the remnants of the blurry vision out of them.

"There is a group that's going to meet us some ways downstream," the man said as he sat upright and began scooping water out of the boat with his hat. "They'll be able to assist you in learning some local customs, what's been afoot and get you on your way to the nearest town called Genoa. They're good fellows but poor so any money that you'll need will have to be obtained by yourself and quickly too."

That took a moment for Corlieu to ingest.

"Get me started? Get me started doing what, why was I awakened this early? Clearly you've moved me from my original sanctuary so you could have done all of this again without rousing me. Are any other members of the Order doing the same?"

The man held up his hands, motioning for Corlieu to relax and keep his voice down.

"We woke you up because you're needed. Some of the other Order members in this region perished but we were able to save you. There's something coming from the east. Genoese merchants returning from the remnants of the Judaea region have come on the vanguard of some terrifying army. Nothing like them since the barbarians overran the old Empire. None of us know what to do."

"…and you expect me to know something?" asked Corlieu shaking his head.

"The army is searching for something judging by the way they plundered the east. Reports indicate that they have certainly set sail by now and will make landfall within this week. The eastern lands they have torn through are diseased and destroyed now and nobody doubts that they will do that to this land unless something is done."

"Indeed, and so you woke me up, plunged me headfirst into water and told me all of this hoping I'd have some clue what to do against this new invading army? The might of the old empire couldn't save itself from invaders and if you awoke me looking for advice, then I doubt there's a strong power anywhere we can rely on."

The man shook his head.

"It's not like that at all. You see, the old barbarians you speak of are human whereas thee are something else."

Corlieu merely looked at the man blankly a moment.

"And you have a reliable source? I'd hardly consider some of the barbarians we faced before to be human."

"The merchants are calling them the Black Plague," he said nodding.

"Then I see the situation," said Corlieu, stretching out and feeling his limbs shakily functioning. "If that's really the case, then I might have a few things that I'll have to do to get ready for this."

"Excellent! Then lay back as I take us the rest of the way to meet the throng. Perchance, you might not have to deal with this alone since word should be spreading to other members, but my master, the Arger of your Sanctuary, told me about the early wake up procedure for your order in times of the utmost emergency. Along with this unnatural disorientation and feebleness, your ability to rapidly learn will be poor and I remember him saying something about a malady of the bowls."

"You jest…right?"

"Wish I was. As he put it, 'you will be digging a lot of holes for some time.'"

Corlieu lay back once again, resting his head underneath his arms. Based on how he felt, he imagined that it must be about 150 years since the caretakers of his order laid him down for his 200 year hibernations. Though he never experienced an early wake up, he was certain that he would be functional enough and in time, everything would be just alright.

Well, I hope…

Chapter 4

Night settled rapidly over the city of Genoa. Once the sun ducked behind the horizon, the offshore wind that was a cooling blessing during the day was reversed, leaving Genoa under the bite of the northern winds. Its wafting tendrils, born from atop the Alps, weaved into every corner and blew quick gusts into any open room. It was now late spring and though the daytime temperature had been steadily rising, the nights were still quite chilly. Anyone outside at this time rushed hurriedly about, eager to escape the wind.

Into this night came two figures, huddled and skirting the walls while spontaneously halting. One of them gestured energetically to a second who came plodding along without the enthusiasm of the first.

"No Corbella, I'm sure we're going the wrong way!" Meliore said, slouching against a wall. "You've been by this part of the street already without anything to show."

Corbella looked wildly around before stopping and jogging over.

"We can't give up. We have found something interesting to do and I don't care how vexed we are, we're too close now to give up!"

Meliore stood up slowly and groaned. She was feeling exhausted and ready to head back to their room. They had been searching for the house that Giacamo told them about for some time, but the directions he gave them proved to be vague enough that they found themselves doubting whether they heard him correctly at all. As they searched on, Meliore's misgivings grew. She had put up a good show pretending to be excited to see what went on, but she was also secretly afraid. Like it or not, Corbella and she were vulnerable and alone without the protection of their families and amongst common people. Even disguised as boys, they might be robbed or killed.

"Let's go home forthwith," she said. "I don't wanna wander around here all night, it's downright frigid and nothing good comes from meandering around."

"Cut your tongue a second," Corbella shot back. "Let me think where we're at and start over again."

Meliore watched her muttering over the directions the shopkeeper gave them and sighed. She looked northwards, towards the mountainside where a few faint lights gleamed in the towers and fortifications. One of those lights belonged to her family's house; right now they would have just finished dinner and would be preparing for bed. A small part of her, especially now, missed it. Lost in the barren low streets of Genoa, the restrictive old life she used to lead felt extremely pleasant and carefree.

"FOR PETER'S SAKE!" said Corbella suddenly, causing Meliore to jump. "It has to be right here! This looks like the place but it doesn't match his descriptions." Corbella slumped down, putting her head in her hands and muttering a steady stream of curses.

Meliore came over to her cousin and crouched down, secretly relieved. Maybe in her fury Corbella would give in and want to head home. It'd be alright, they probably weren't missing anything anyways. She put her hand on Corbella's shoulder and leaned her head against the wall.

"Do you hear that!?" Meliore said. She was so startled at the noise that she forgot to consider whether or not she should say anything.

"What are you talking about? I don't hear anything," said Corbella, lifting her head and looking skeptically at Meliore.

"I…mean," she stuttered before realizing there was no way to cover her blunder. "Very well, just put your ear on the wall here," she said, pulling Corbella over and pressing her face against the wall.

Corbella looked disgruntled for a moment before a big grin broke across her face.

"I hear talking and yelling, oh glorious sound of revelry, you have two new friends!"

"Therein is the right place after all," said Meliore with a sigh of resignation. "How do we get in?"

"We just go 'round and knock on the door I'm guessing," she said, getting up and running around the corner.

Corbella ran off and flailed her limbs in wild excitement, turning the corner before Meliore could even stand.

"Wait, stop!" she said, scrambling against the wall and tearing off after Corbella. *"Don't leave me here you clod!"*

She ran around, catching glimpses of Corbella ahead of her. Meliore caught up as they neared the front of the house and together they walked up to the door. There in the window was a solitary, shaded lamp. From here, it was impossible to tell that anything was going on. They approached the door slowly and Meliore was suddenly grasped with doubt. Her breathing slowed and she could feel her heart hammering away at her chest.

"Quick," said Corbella, turning around and reaching up for her hat. "Take a gander at me, will our disguises suffice? And remember the names we made up! This is not the place to go calling me Corbella."

Meliore had only a moment of inspecting Corbella in the moonlight before they heard a sudden onrush of heavy footsteps from inside the room. She froze, looking up over Corbella in time to see the wooden door fly open and come crashing into them. Meliore had little notion of what happened. The impact threw both of them off balance and they barely caught themselves before a loud deep voice was yelling from the doorway. It was only when she regained her senses did she understand what was happening.

"I TOLD YOU, IF E'ER YOU SHOWED UP HERE AGAIN, BEGGING AND ANNOYING CUSTOMERS LIKE THAT, THAT'D BE THE END OF YOU!" shouted a bald, heavyset man from the doorway.

The man he was yelling at went toppling by as though he was thrown and laid squirming in the street. He got to his hands and knees, crawling a few paces back towards the door.

"Just a bit longer, you know I'm good for it," he said, groveling on the ground. "Hardly my fault that the boss is late with my pay."

"HARDLY IS IT MY FAULT EITHER. YOU KNOW THE RULES: NO MONEY, GET OUT!"

The man went to close the door but stopped short. It was this moment when he caught sight of the girls sprawled to the side.

"What are you two doing 'ere?"

"We're here to join the throng!" said Corbella jumping to her feet and dragging Meliore up with her.

"So you are, who invited you two?" said the man, looking suspiciously at them.

"A fella at the docks," said Corbella a little meekly. "Goes by the name of Giacamo."

The man gave a laugh and waved them towards the open door. "I know who you're talking about, indeed he's already down here and quite off his head if you get what I mean. Very well, come on in my young lads....eh, what are your names?"

"I'm Melio.."

A sharp jab at her ribs from Corbella made her stop sharply and cough.

"Never you mind you two, come in forthwith and watch your step there Melio if that is what you call yourself," said the man, motioning to the open door. "Funny name, and tis too chilly out here. I'd rather not have new guests catch something evil off the wind tonight."

"Wait," said the groveling man, crawling forward on the ground. "You'll let them in and not me?"

"You two have money, right?" asked the man holding the door open. Both Meliore and Corbella slapped their pockets, producing the tinkle of coins. He smiled and turned back to the man crawling towards him.

"There you go, they mayst enter," he said and closed the door.

It was dark for a moment then a lamp was uncovered and in it, Meliore could see that they were in a large and roughly furnished shop. Wooden tables and benches lined the walls and sawdust littered the floor.

"My name is Gennaro, this is my house and workshop. As long as you don't get too out of hand or bother the others, then you're welcomed here when'ver we have our little celebrations. Follow me...," he said, turning and walking across the room and down a flight of stairs.

The girls followed him, hearing the din of laughter and noises grow as they descended the stairs.

"What made you hit me?" whispered Meliore angrily.

"We're supposed to be boys, remember? What boy do you know who's named Meliore?"

"You still didn't have to hit me," she said, rubbing her tender side.

At the bottom of the flight of stairs, Gennaro threw open a door and ushered the girls in. The sudden brightness and burst of noise was startling. She had never seen so many jovial strangers together before. A group of dock workers were crowded around a bar at the right, stooped over, talking slowly and making tired gestures to each other. Behind them sat a few foreign merchants around a table. They were dressed in unusual looking lengthy clothes and their faces were intent as they conversed with each other. A smoky haze issued from their midst and their drinks were scarcely touched.

It was to the left, however, that most of the commotion came. Tables of men facing each other, talking excitedly would break into sudden mixtures of yelling and cheering faces accompanied by many more frustrated and cursing ones.

"Are they gambling?" asked Meliore, watching a group sulkily pass money around and glare at each other for bursting into wild claims. "I thought gambling wasn't allowed?"

Gennaro laughed and waved the girls over to follow him towards the counter.

"Gambling is perfectly legal, even under the church. It's the fact that gambling promotes behavior of this type and worse that they don't like," he said, gesturing towards the figures at the bar.

"I don't understand," said Corbella.

"The drunkenness, the fighting and general unrest that seems to come from a place like this. It's damned well difficult trying to avoid the scrutiny of the city and the church. Hence why I have to be so strict."

The girls came up and took seats. Gennaro pulled out a flagon and poured the girls some wine and held out his hand. It wasn't till after Corbella paid him that he pushed their wine towards them and continued talking.

"This place is more of a local hangout, you know? I'm just a friendly neighbor who happens to have access to a lot of wine. Most of it is homemade, unfortunately. Tonight how'ver, I happened to get some really good stuff at a great price too."

One of the slouched figures nearby crawled up and looked dizzily at them.

"This grand stuff, courtesy of that botched wedding the other day. Did 'a hear about that? The finest in drink and food to be had and it was all for naught!"

"Not for nothing!" shouted a livelier figure sitting further down. "…no chance of getting our hands on something the likes of this for the price! Heavens bless those girls, right?"

"They gave those Venetians the slip! Good for them!" said another low voice.

Gennaro shook his head and looked towards the girls again.

"I don't know what t'make of it and I'll bet that I'm probably not going t'be far off the mark. I was there at that wedding, tending t'the after–ceremonies when the Venetians came out. They were in a scary state of mind, you know?"

Meliore nodded and strained to keep her eagerness under control. She couldn't believe it, the people here were celebrating and thanking them. She hastily tried to disguise her smile behind her drink, but it was impossible with Gennaro facing her.

"I dunno what you're grinning at," he said, looking straight into Meliore's eyes. "Ah me! Hardly do we like those Venetians anyways, but they mean war if ever I had t'guess it."

Again, Gennaro sighed and straightened up slowly. His name was being yelled and he picked up his flagon and walked towards them.

"Oh, one other thing," he said turning back to the girls. "Don't do anything brash or stupid and I won't have to throw you out, you know?"

Meliore nodded and watched him go before turning towards Corbella.

"What do you make of this?" Meliore asked.

"Let's move a little more out of the way. I don't want anyone o'er hearing us," Corbella said, picking up her flagon and trying a sip. "Ugg, you know I ne'er liked this stuff."

"Just nurture it, you don't have to down the whole thing," Meliore said while trying some. She must have grimaced at the awful taste because Corbella smirked at her and walked over to the corner near the entrance.

"War?" she said to Meliore. "I just wanted to escape marrying that ugly guy, never would I have guessed that we'd start a war."

"Give me peace a second; wouldst they start a war over something the likes of this? I mean, you heard that guy. He hardly knew what to make of it all. Why are you so worried?"

"I didn't like my family but I didn't want all of them killed!" Said Corbella a little forcefully.

"Calm yourself," said Meliore, putting a hand on her shoulder and looking nervously at the nearby table. The merchants there had turned around at Corbella's outburst but had swiftly gone back to their discussion. The significance of Corbella's sentence went unheard.

"They have a plan for things like this," Meliore continued. "No chance our families are at risk in case a war broke. There are soldiers to hire for something like that. My family was never dumb enough to fight on their own and I'll wager that our families would work together if there were to be any trouble with the Venetians."

"You think?" asked Corbella, absentmindedly taking a sip of her wine.

"I'm pretty sure of it. Now com'ere, let's see what's going with the gamblers."

Meliore walked towards the tables, standing at a distance and watching the groups of men. One by one, tables erupted into noise and money exchanged hands while gamblers argued. And then they settled down, sitting in silent concentration, and pondered their chances.

"We have a few empty seats," said a man at one table against the corner. He was looking and waving them over. "C'mon o'er and give it a shot!"

As Meliore walked closer, she saw that the man who called them over was strangely dressed, even compared to the merchants. He also held a significant portion of the money at the table. His eyes glinted in the lamplight, making Meliore pause. She didn't like his look, it was like something she had only seen in wild animals. It was the look of a predator sitting amidst a group of fallen prey. The men around the table were glum and defeated.

Why are they continuing to play if they're losing?

"Well," said the man, breaking Meliore's thoughts. "Are you boys in or not?"

Not used to being addressed as boys, Meliore stuttered a second before Corbella cut in.

"I'm in," she shouted, pulling out a chair and plunking her drink down. "I've played often with stall grooms and I know a few things about dice games."

The other men around the table looked over, their spiritual dirge disrupted by

Corbella's eagerness, and chuckled.

"You'd better be careful Corlieu," said the guy sitting to his right. "This young fellow has barely touched the drink and he's strivin' for your ill-gotten gains."

"Oh, no reason for worrying too much," the man, apparently named Corlieu, said, looking at Corbella. "Hardly does it matter the tricks our new guest has, you can't influence a good game of hazard."

"Corbella," whispered Meliore, lowering herself close to her ear. "We never played hazard before, do you know what to do?"

"It's not my turn, I hope. I'll figure it out quickly. Trust me and stop calling me by my name!"

"But we don't have much money either. Don't get reckless or else we will really be in trouble."

"I realize that. I won't bet much and if I lose I'll say something about getting another drink."

Meliore looked down at Corbella's barely touched drink and felt her innards tighten slightly. They weren't going to believe that and if Corbella lost them a lot of money, they might be living on the street very soon. She looked up and across the table at Corlieu. He was squinting at her with his head cocked to one side. It was not an evil look, but it was disquieting all the same. Meliore could feel herself take a deep breath as his eyes stared into her. For a moment, she thought his eyebrows went up and his mouth hung open, but before she knew it the round had already started and the moment had passed.

Straightening up, Corlieu produced a set of dazzlingly ornate dice and handed two of them over to the man next him. He held them tightly, took a breath and cast them.

"Ah, a main of eight," he said, throwing a coin to a small pile in the middle of the table. "Why did I stay? That's my most unlucky of numbers. Give me the dice again and let's have the end of this."

He rolled the dice again and everyone at the table leaned over in anticipation.

"FIVE!" he said. "Alright, I'm still alive!"

Immediately around the table, the other men leaned over and started talking to each other. One of them leaned over to Corbella, taking a big drink of his wine and looking at her.

"I bet he still won't throw in," the man said, sliding a coin between himself and Corbella. "Care to bet otherwise?"

Corbella glanced behind her towards Meliore and mouthed, "What do I do?" Meliore simply shrugged, she didn't know what the best thing to do was. She was still trying to figure out the rules of the game and was simply glad that it wasn't her stuck there.

"I'll bet that he does roll his main," said Corbella extremely awkwardly, sliding a coin against his.

"Excellent!" said the man, grinning and looking back across the table.

"You all about done?" asked the man, impatiently rolling the dice from one hand to the other.

Everyone at the table nodded and the man let the dice roll across the table. All of their heads tipped forward and Meliore could feel herself stand on her toes and peer over Corbella's head. There was an odd combination of a few sighs of relief and a louder chorus of long witted cursing. The man had apparently failed to roll a winning number and everyone that bet in his favor, including Corbella, had lost.

The dice passed to the next person at the table and the process repeated again. Meliore watched, shifting from foot to foot and taking another gulp of her drink. Corbella was having horrible luck and after two more straight rounds of losing, threw her hands up in frustration.

"I don't get it!" she said, looking at Meliore. "This doesn't seem to be a hard game, but I just can't win anything!"

"Let me have one turn at it," said Meliore, putting her hand on the back of Corbella's chair and giving it a tug.

"You have one round," Corbella said, standing up and giving Meliore a coin.

The men at the table laughed and punched Corbella on the arm as she walked away. She looked thoroughly irritated and muttered something about food and drink. Another of the men left the table, exchanging goodnights with some of the others and leaving with a sneer at Corlieu. Much to Meliore's astonishment, the guy next to her placed the set of dice in her hands.

"Your turn," Corlieu said.

"Wait, what?" said Meliore, looking around the table in astonishment. "I just joined; can't I pass or something?"

Everyone at the table ignored her and busied themselves counting their money. Only Corlieu was looking at her.

"It's your turn, this game isn't complicated," he said. "Simply pick a number: five, nine or anything 'twixt the two. Then throw out your bet, make sure we're all ready and roll the dice again."

Meliore gulped and looked down at the dice. She was concentrating on trying to figure out what number she should pick and slowly got distracted by the dice. They were elegantly carved, perfectly square and lined with an elegant black and gold design. She had never seen anything so ornate and intricate. The lamplight reflected sparks and shooting stars across their surface, utterly captivating her in their mesmerizing structure.

"Well," said Corlieu curtly. The whole table was ready and looking at her.

"Five!" she said.

Everybody nodded and Meliore took a breath and rolled the dice. As they rolled, she noticed Corlieu was looking at her with a hard stare.

"Eight!" a man said. Once again, everyone at the table turned and started arranging their various side bets. Meliore was left awkwardly waiting for everyone to finish. Throughout this time, she occasionally caught Corlieu staring at her and occasionally glancing down at the dice. When everyone was ready, she rolled again.

The table fell hushed and many of the men fell agape. Corlieu was staring down at the dice and he then looked up at Meliore in amazement.

"Good roll, you threw in," he said.

"I threw what?" started Meliore.

"He means you won you clod," said the guy next to her.

"AND THE REST OF US LOST!" said another man, throwing a handful of money to the middle of the table. "The only good bet I thought I had all night and you had to go and spoil it!"

Meliore looked around puzzled. Most of the table had soured a little and were counting what was left of their money. She hadn't noticed till now, but everybody had made pretty sizable bets against her so her winnings were substantial.

"Don't worry," said Corlieu from across the table. "They're like this every time someone pulls off something miraculous. I should know, we're the only two to have done something like this in a while." As he said this, he pulled together a small pile of loose coins. "Thanks, I bet on you. Take your money and pass the dice."

A large portion of the pile at the middle was shifted to her and Meliore gathered it together in astonishment. It was amazing; she won it all so quickly and without really even knowing what she was doing. Should she stay and maybe lose it all?

"Whoa, look at all that!" said Corbella, walking up and whacking Meliore on the back. "That's amazing, you just won that?"

All Meliore could do in response was produce a half–hearted smile and shrug.

Chapter 5

Never before had Meliore known anything she was this good at. After that first nervous hand, she found herself steadily making more and more money. There were times when she decided to take wild gambles and found the limits of her luck that night as the other gamblers reveled in finally winning at her expense. Even then, it was amazing. When some of the men cut their losses and left, Corbella decided to try and have another go at it, but with three straight losses, she gave up and resigned herself to watching and cheering Meliore on.

Midnight had long past and it wouldn't be more than a few more hours before the sun peeked over the eastern horizon. Gennaro's place had quieted down significantly at this time. There were some sleeping figures strewn across the tables and all of the other gamblers had gone at this point. There seemed to be only one person who was having more luck than Meliore and that was Corlieu. Pretty soon, they were the last ones left.

"You say that you've never played this game before, right?" asked Corlieu suddenly. The corner of his eyebrow twitched in as he looked at Meliore.

"I suppose I already gave it away earlier, but no. I learned some other games of dice before but never one like Hazard."

"Teach me if you please. Let's play one of those other ones that you know," said Corlieu after staring and nodding off for a bit. "What's it called?"

Meliore opened her mouth for a moment and shut it again. Considering that it was one of her favorite two player games, she knew she ought to have remembered.

"Quick," she asked, turning to her side to face Corbella who had her arms folded and was resting her chin on the table. "What is that game called? You know which one, the one I always played where we have the pair of dice each."

Corbella looked at her blankly for a moment.

"You're the one who played it, not me. How am I supposed to know?"

"Forget it," said Corlieu suddenly with a bemused expression. "the name doesn't matter I suppose. Do you remember how to play it?"

"Certainly yes," said Meliore. "Give me two of your dice and take two for yourself."

Corlieu did this, slowly selecting a pair of dice and rolling them across the table.

"We lay out a beginning bet, roll our dice and keep them covered. Don't let me see yours," Meliore said. "Then, look at your dice and we gamble on who has the higher number."

"And what happens when we tie?"

"The money stays and goes to the next winner."

Corlieu sunk back in his chair and thought about this a moment. For a second, he pulled his hands off his dice as if to rest his chin on them, but he hurriedly covered them back up with a suspicious glance at Corbella.

"Don't worry, I didn't see," Corbella said.

"Alright, let's do this," said Corlieu, tossing out two coins.

Meliore did the same and they both looked at each other. Corlieu was staring hard at her. His eyes were not unsettling, but Meliore was getting the sensation that he was thinking hard about something.

"Eleven!" said Meliore, picking up her hand.

Corlieu did likewise. He rolled an 11 as well.

"Again," he said, picking up his dice and rolling them in his hands before slamming them down on the table.

Meliore did likewise. Looking, she held her composure as she saw a pair of sixes. This time however, Corlieu threw four coins to the center of the table. Meliore matched with four of her own and when they were ready, they removed their hands.

Corlieu rolled a 12.

"Again!" said Corlieu, repeating the process.

A third time, Meliore repeated the move. She saw Corbella sitting next to her nervously looking at them, but she didn't care. Her luck had not failed her seriously that night and she felt a rush of confidence come from within her.

"My luck won't let me down."

A second time, they both rolled elevens. This time, Corlieu broke his vigil and looked suspiciously at Meliore.

"What could he be looking at?" she thought with a gulp. "I haven't done anything wrong; does he think I'm cheating?"

As she thought about it, a blond hair unwound itself from the careful braid she had made and slipped down across her face. The dull red gleam of the lamps caught the strand of it, causing it to glisten with an auburn sparkle. Meliore gasped. Corlieu had noticed too and was slowly standing up. Corbella seemed to know that something was amiss and was standing up as well.

It was at this point that three things happened in quick succession. A flicker of fire through a small window caught their attention. The orange flame suddenly burst into life as the building across the street caught fire followed by a shattering sound as a window broke. A torch came crashing in the center of the room and immediately set the central tables ablaze.

*****

As soon as the torch broke through the window, Corlieu made a move to sweep up all the money on the table. Corbella, who was a little quicker than Meliore lunged and rammed him at an angle. He lost his balance and fell to one side.

"*WE'RE UNDER ATTACK!*" yelled Gennaro from behind the bar. "*EVERYBODY GET OUT!*"

There was a rush as the remainder of the occupants flooded the exits. They were yelling and cursing; a few tried for the window and managed to scramble out. In a matter of seconds, only three people remained.

"*What are you doing Corlieu!*" shouted Corbella, coughing from the sudden influx of smoke.

Corlieu said nothing, he rolled to his back and kicked a chair at her. It clipped her in the legs and she stumbled to the floor. Her hair came out of the hat and her loose braid came undone. Between the table legs, she saw him back on his feet and bending over the table. Without losing a moment, she crouched and pushed the table, pinning him between it and the nearby wall. With some satisfaction she heard a grunt as the air got knocked out of him.

"NOT A CHANCE!" she yelled, grabbing his legs and pulling him down. *"WE NEED THAT COINAGE TO LIVE!"*

Corlieu twisted and landed hard on his back, but sprang up into a crouch and looked her dead in the eyes.

"You don't understand me little lady," he yelled over the roar of the spreading fire. He held up his bag and it clinked with the coins. Somehow he had already cleaned the table. *"I need these too. Far more than your simple lives depends on it."*

It was at this point that Meliore suddenly appeared.

"I'LL SHOW YOU SIMPLE!" she yelled, snatching the bag out of his hands. She then stood up, colliding with the table and sending it rolling over onto both Corbella and Corlieu. Meliore then dashed over the burning wreckage towards the stairway, but an arrow flew through the broken window and caught the bag clean out of her hand and pinning it against the far wall.

The three of them made a dash for it. Meliore, being the closest got there first but the arrow was solidly lodged and Corlieu was hot on her tracks. With one giant heave, the bag tore loose and a rainbow of coins and dice followed in its wake as the bag went flying across the room. It landed forcefully on Corbella's face, covering it and causing her to reel from the pain and struggle to pull it off for a second as she lost her footing. Her arms spiraled outwards and she heard Corlieu shout as she crashed into him. She felt his hand pull the bag off of her face just as a giant cracking sound came from above. The roof splintered and was caving in right on top of her, but most unexpectedly Corlieu yanked her off her feet and out of the way. She skidded over, into Meliore who was coming in her direction and the two rammed into each other and rolled against the wall. Corbella was dazed and swore as she caught the blurred image of Corlieu running up the stairway.

"MELIORE!" she yelled, knocking aside the furniture to get to her cousin. *"WE'VE GOT TO GET OUT OF HERE!"*

She went over and helped her up. The impact however, was severe enough that she moved with difficulty. Together, they scrambled up the stairs to the entrance of Gennaro's building. Through the broken windows, they could see many fires and hear the sounds of combat. With some trepidation, Corbella opened the door and they hobbled out into the street.

All around them, they saw Venetian soldiers running and setting buildings alight. A few people were fighting back, but there was no seriously organized defense just yet. There seemed to be no safe place to go.

"Corbella," said Meliore, slumping to the floor. "Everything's alight! Where now shall we go?"

Back and forth, Corbella looked desperately. Smoke filled the street and her head ached terribly.

"I don't know," she said looking around in alarm as the entrance of Gennaro's building erupted in flames. "We're trapped between fire and enemies!"

"THERE, LOOK!" shouted Meliore, pointing at something through the smoke.

A troop of horsemen rode up, scattering a pillaging group of Venetians. One of them rode down the street, giving orders to the others and surveying the damage. He rode in the direction of Corbella and stopped twenty feet away. A sudden gust of wind cleared the smoke and she saw to her horror that it was none other than Alessandro, Meliore's brother. He pointed at them, his mouth flapping uselessly for a moment.

"YOU!" he finally managed to stammer. *"YOU BOTH…HERE…I DON'T BELIEVE IT! I KNEW YOU WEREN'T KIDNAPPED. OH FATHER'S GOING TO HAVE A GREAT SURPRISE FOR YOU WHEN I TAKE YOU HOME!"*

It was at this point that Corbella noticed another shape riding through the smoke. It was closing from behind Alessandro quickly and did not have the look of a soldier. The rider wore a long brimmed hat, his horse was small and lean and from its sides flopped a considerable amount of baggage. It was Corlieu. He emerged from the smoke, riding at a full gallop and from his side he pulled out a small stick and swung its end straight across the rear of Alessandro's horse. That horse immediately threw a rear and went bucking off down the street, eventually throwing him into a pile of debris.

Throwing the stick away and continuing to gallop through the flames, Corlieu leaned towards Corbella and tilted his hat as he rode by.

"THANK YOU GENEROUS HOSTESSES!" he yelled, riding off down the street and disappearing into the smoke.

Too astonished to know what to do, Corbella helped Meliore stand up again and she pursed her lips as she looked in Corlieu's direction.

"Was that my brother? And… *CORLIEU?!*" Meliore shouted, pulling herself off of Corbella and shaking her head.

Corbella couldn't do anything but stare off in the direction that he vanished in. In all the years of her life, she had never been cheated like this. The shock of watching the perpetrator getting away after the fight Meliore and she endured was simply staggering. She didn't know what to do.

"C'mon," said Meliore, tugging at Corbella. "We have to get out of here. If that was my brother and he comes back, we're doomed!"

Gradually the rage burnt itself out and Corbella began to think clearly again. They were still in a lot of danger. Burning buildings aside, there were soldiers running around in the smoke and none of them were their allies. She thought for a moment, trying to figure out a safe place to hide.

"Help!" came a voice from one of the buildings. "Don't just stand there like a pair of dolts, help me you two!"

Corbella turned and saw Gennaro trying to claw his way out of a tiny window in his burning building. His semi–corpulent figure had tightened around the edge and he was helpless. Smoke was pouring out from the sides of the window he was stuck in.

They made their way over as quickly as they could, grabbing him by the hands and dislodging him from the window. He crawled a few paces away and sat for a moment, panting and unresponsive. Though his shirt and arms were scratched from his struggle, his legs and shoes were black from smoke. He waved her off when she tried to help and instead was relegated to sitting and catching his breath.

"Many thanks," he said after a moment, getting up slowly and shaking out his legs. "My backsides were nearly roasted while you two were watching the melee."

A burning timber fell a few feet away from them and kicked up a tremendous plume of dust and glowing embers against them.

"Come with me gents!" he said, picking up a painful looking hobble and waving them after him as he went jogging down the street. "I know of a safe house we can hide in."

 Without any other clue what to do, they followed after him. After a few minutes, it became apparent that Gennaro would not be able to make it so

Corbella found Meliore and herself supporting him as best as they could. It was tricky work and they went slowly. Not only was Gennaro a tremendous burden but the Venetians were renewing their assault against the defenders and nobody was particularly careful who they attacked or where their arrows went. At one point, they took refuge in a burnt out building and were stuck as they watched a large group of Venetians launching an attack on the defending Genoans.

"How much further is there to go?" asked Corbella, leaning over and speaking directly into Gennaro's ear.

"Merely a few houses further and one up. Might'a been there by now if it wasn't for all this!"

"What can we do in the meantime, is there a way around it?"

"Just sit tight and hope this building doesn't collapse."

Both Corbella and Meliore made moves to look up but Gennaro pushed their heads back down.

"Don't look, it's better not to know. Should it come down on us, we hopefully won't even know until we meet St. Peter."

"Lovely," said Meliore. "I'm going to strangle you up there if that happens!"

Corbella saw Gennaro smirk nervously. She shook her head and looked back out at the street. The fighting was spreading in their direction. Though she was fairly certain that the soldiers would stay confined to the street, she couldn't be certain. If the fighting did spread to their location, then they would be cut off from their safe house. Their only option would be to head back into the burning buildings.

Their luck held out however. A fresh wave of Genoan soldiers successfully pushed the attackers down the street and towards the harbor. For the moment, everything was clear.

"Now for it!" said Gennaro, launching himself out of their hiding spot and sprinting down the street as best he could.

Corbella easily caught up and dogged his tracks while scanned around for enemies. They had survived an awful lot of close calls that night and she certainly didn't want to be in this situation when their luck ran out.

"Quick, in here!" said Gennaro, pushing open a section of fence and heading down an ally. They followed, running down a tight lane and finally saw him disappear into a building while waving them in. Once inside, he shut the door.

"Let…let me catch my breath a moment," he said. "There are some candles here, but I need to find where my tinder box is."

Corbella breathed a sigh of relief and sat down on the floor with her back against the wall. It was cool, slightly damp and wonderfully soothing. She didn't realize how much the constant heat from the fire took out of her. Her face and hands were flush and tender, everything had the smell of the burnt buildings and she had to endure coughing fits from all the smoke. She felt Meliore slump down next to her.

"We made it, I can hardly believe it," said Meliore. She coughed a few minutes too before clearing her throat and suddenly laughing. "We're alive! But what on earth do we do now? Our inn is probably burnt down, my money was stolen by Corlieu and we probably look horrid."

The sounds of striking tinder caught Corbella's attention for a moment. A flame emerged and caught a set of candles alight revealing Gennaro's face. He walked over and handed them each a candle.

"Corlieu did you say? How do you know of him?" he asked, placing his candle on a table and pulling a chair over. "Wait, you're those boys from tonight right? Yes, I recognize your clothes, but you're girls! What in Peter's name were you doing dressed as boys?"

Sheepishly, the girls looked at each other and then back again at Gennaro.

"We've been disguised as boys since we got here," said Meliore. "I didn't think you'd let us in if we were girls and it has been the best way of avoiding attention."

Gennaro snorted in laughter.

"Women are allowed!" he said. "Not many come, but you would've been treated relatively the same in there. "A couple ladies were slumped down at the bar and on the tables too. Didn't you see them?"

Corbella opened her mouth to say something, but all she could manage was a shrug. She felt as though they went through a lot of trouble and preparation that whole evening for nothing. Again Gennaro laughed and got up.

"It's alright, no harm. Now what is this about Corlieu? You were gambling with him, weren't you?"

"Yes, that was us," said Meliore. "When someone threw the torch through the window, he made a grab for the money. We started fighting and he managed to escape with almost all of it."

"…almost all of it? You mean you got some?" said Corbella.

Meliore pulled off her coat and turned it upside down. From its pockets, there fell out some coins. It was a bare fraction of the amount that was on the table, but it was something. Lastly, a pair of dice fell out and rolled across the table.

"The dice!" Meliore said in amazement. "I forgot I got those. Are they yours Gennaro?"

He shook his head, walking over with a drink in his hand.

"No, those aren't mine. All gamblers are responsible for bringing in their own equipment. Those must belong to Corlieu."

"All the time I was fighting him Meliore, you were busy getting the dice?" Corbella said indignantly. "I could 'a used your help you know! Maybe we would have gotten more than just this pittance. Why did you get those anyways?"

Meliore shrugged and looked embarrassed.

"I don't know. They're beautiful, have you ever seen anything like them before?"

Corbella sighed and rested her head on her knees. They were nearly broke, without a place to stay and their cover was ruined.

"What now for you two?" asked Gennaro. "I get the feeling that you are in some type of local trouble."

"Yes, we are," said Meliore. "You know about that wedding a couple of weeks ago you had mentioned, where the bride ditched her Venetian husband to be?"

Gennaro nodded a moment, then his eyes widened in amazement.

"THAT WAS YOU?" he yelled, looking at Meliore.

"That was me," said Corbella picking up one hand.

"Oh dear me… then you two have really stepped in it I see. What are you going to do then?"

"I want to chase after Corlieu," hissed Corbella angrily.

"Why? What are you going to do that for?" asked Gennaro incredulously. "He's long gone by now, on his way to Marseilles or so he said earlier in the evening."

"I want revenge," Corbella said. "Nobody gets away with that. He took a lot of money and got away. We almost died in the building too thanks to him. We have to!"

"Be careful going out and looking for revenge," said Gennaro after thinking a moment. "It can get you in worse trouble than you're already in."

"What worse trouble is there? It's not like there's anything we can do here anymore. Her brother," she said, motioning to Meliore, "knows we're here and will be telling our families first chance he gets. Soon, we won't be able to get a bite to eat without someone recognizing us."

Gennaro nodded for a moment before slapping his knees and standing up.

"Fair point there. I don't know what your families would do to either of you if you got caught, but it won't be pretty. You two can stay here for a few nights if you wish so you can make some plans. There are some cots in the room to your right."

"What is this place?" asked Meliore.

"It's one of my storage buildings. I always keep a room or two in them in case I have to work late or host some business partners. Nobody'll disturb you, I'll see to that."

He turned around, exchanging weary "goodnights" with the girls and waving off their thankful overtones before passing through the doorway.

As they made their way towards the room Gennaro indicated, Corbella stopped at the doorway and put a hand up.

"We have only two ways to go from here," she said looking at Meliore. "We need to go back to our home grounds but what we do there will be all the difference. Meliore, are we going to turn ourselves in and give up?"

Meliore looked back at her in shock. It was clear she never expected something like this to come from Corbella.

"Go back?" she said, taking a step back and leaning against the doorway. "We're going back home?"

"No, I am simply asking what you want to do. I am the one who goaded you into coming and brought us to the sorry state we're now in."

Corbella hung her head down and looked off to the side. Perhaps it was due to growing up around her so much, but Corbella was certain she could feel a strong desire to go home. Meliore still had that ability, she would only get in minor trouble. The more Corbella thought about it, the more she realized there was no returning home for her. This decision was for Meliore alone.

"What are you going to do if I go home?" Meliore asked after a moment.

"I cannot go back home," she said. "Not after what I did."

"Then neither can I, cousin!" Meliore exclaimed. "I do miss the comfort and routine at home, but whatever shall I do without you?"

"But Meliore…," started Corbella looking up at her.

"There's nothing more to be said," interrupted Meliore, clapping her on the shoulders. "Heaven knows I'll regret it sometimes, but I know deep down that I will regret abandoning you here more than anything in the wide world."

"Thanks Meliore," said Corbella. She felt a knot of tension she never knew existed unwind in her chest. She suddenly lunged at her cousin in a mighty hug. "Thanks a lot!"

"Whoa, alright I get the sentiment," said Meliore stumbling around a moment. "I am not going anywhere, so what shall we do now? It sounded like you had a plan."

"I do," said Corbella. She released herself and stood back against the wall. "I am positive that we can get some supplies from Gennaro. We won't need too much and we still have his favor. If we can get that from him, all we need are our horses."

"Our horses?" Meliore asked, sounding hopeful. "You mean we're going back to get our horses?"

"Of course, none better than our own! We'll find that thief on Mercurie and Stoccata."

They walked into the room in higher spirits collapsed on the nearest bed. It was nicely furnished and Corbella's bed was amazingly comfortable. Every muscle ached as she slipped between the blankets. Bruises pulsed on almost every limb, but she didn't care. She was so tired that sleep took her before she could say or do anything. Inexorable, unavoidable, she drifted off without a struggle mere seconds after lying down.

They slept into most of the next day. By the time they woke up, they found that the sun had already passed its apex and all the smoldering fires were out in the lower portions of the city. Even from the ground, Corbella could see that Meliore's fears were correct and their previous lodging was burnt. She did not fancy digging through the wreckage either to look for anything that might have escaped the Venetian torches. With no other prospect and the urge for revenge still hot in her heart, Corbella formulated a plan for how they were going to sneak into their family's livery barn and run off with their horses.

Corbella was certain that it would be rather easy. Not only did they know the groom's routines but since it was where they spent a majority of time they knew exactly where everything was, even in the darkness.

Or so she thought.

"Curses," whispered Meliore who was laying down next to Corbella in the tree line just outside the stables. *"Why is that portion of the stables lit? What's going on I wonder?"*

"Indeed," said Corbella biting her lip nervously. *"Maybe one of the horses is injured? He can't work in total darkness you know."*

"It looks like there are too many people over there. Surely it would be something that the farrier and maybe one groom could take care of without a crowd."

Corbella looked a moment longer before realizing that Meliore was correct. There was a large gathering inside the barn and now they were moving about hurriedly and the sound of horses walking forward reached her ears. Before she could do anything other than gape, a group of eight riders set off down the path towards Genoa.

"It's Alessandro and he's on Mercurie!" hissed a frantic Meliore. *"Did you see, did*

they take Stocatta too?"

"I couldn't tell, they were bunched up but it didn't look like any greys were among them," she said, speaking in a normal voice as her heart dropped.

"What shall we do about Mercurie, do we wait for them to return?"

"No, we can't. They might not be back till the morning and then what? We'll need to wait the entire day again before trying this. In the meantime, Corlieu keeps on getting further away and we risk getting ourselves caught by staying around Genoa."

She stood up and stretched a second before tugging on Meliore to follow after her. Together they crossed the plain leading up to the barn. The bag of supplies bounced annoyingly against her back and slowed her run. For those seconds, Corbella felt horribly exposed and continuously glanced down the path where Alessandro had gone. As they reached the wall, the light inside was extinguished. She heard scuffling and footsteps going up the breezeway.

Corbella crouched and closed her eyes. The wall they were leaning against was flat without a trace of bushes or debris to hid in. The footsteps went up slowly and around the corner away from them. Everything was silent for a few more moments before she heard a door creak open and slam.

"I guess now is the best time," said Meliore. Immediately after saying this, a nicker came from a nearby stall and a grey nose stuck out from an opening in the wall.

Meliore ran over with a squeal and scratched his nose.

"Who moved you over here boy, this isn't your home!"

"C'mon," said Corbella nervously looking back down the trail. *"Keep your voice down now and let's get a move on."*

They both crept around and into the tack room. As quickly and quietly as they could, they gathered all the equipment they needed. Luckily, the sound of horses occasionally kicking the walls in the other aisle covered their movement. They knew at any point however, the groom could come out and happen upon them.

"Quickly," said Corbella opening the stall door. It creaked sharply and she froze in horror, listening for the sounds of the groom leaving his room. Nothing happened though and she breathed a sigh of relief.

They both hastily tacked up Stoccata and led him out of the stall. As they were leaving, Corbella heard a door creak open in the other aisle. At this same time, the horse's hipbone caught the side of the wall and the impact shook the barn and caused him to sidestep a moment. His hooves echoed loudly.

"C'mon!" said Meliore, jumping atop Stoccata and reaching down to help Corbella up. The groom was fully alert now and they him running over. Corbella scrambled on, hampered by the bag of supplies and frantically trying to keep up with the moving horse. She leapt up and scrambled on, climbing up the saddle like a squirrel and wrapping her arms around Meliore's waist. They cantered off just as the room came around the corner. Corbella saw the whites of his eyes as the horse came charging at him and he dove to one side.

"Don't head for the trail," said Corbella holding tight.

"I'm no fool, I'll take us the opposite way through the trees. What do you think they're going to do though?"

Corbella looked behind her and saw the shape of the groom running off towards the main house.

"There goes our unnoticed escape," she said with a groan. "It is fortunate that we rested today, we're going to have to get as far away as possible."

"ALRIGHT CORLIEU, WE'RE COMING FOR YOU!" yelled Meliore as they disappeared into the tree-line.

Chapter 6

Dusk was creeping across the valley, spreading deepening shadows amongst the surrounding woods and welcoming a cold w wind from the old Roman Sea many miles to the south.

Corlieu sat, wrapped in a layer of fur and huddled up to his fire. Nearby, tied to a low limb but still able to reach the ground grazed his horse. This region was much colder than he remembered from his previous reincarnation and the grazing would keep the horse warm while Corlieu sat and pondered what to do next. Though he remembered the tactics the legionaries used to keep from freezing at night, it was unnerving being alone without the army of Gaul in this dangerous land… if it was as dangerous as it used to be, that is.

What for the Emperor's sake could I hope to accomplish here? These little kingdoms and fractious armies will ne'er withstand this force of shades out of the past.

He didn't know. Usually, members of the order wake up around the same time and can rely on the assistance of the sanctuary to help acclimate themselves to the surrounding world. Corlieu was awakened unceremoniously and ejected into the nearby river. The effects of an early wakeup were having a tremendous effect on him. He did not have the ability to rapidly absorb information and it took much longer than usual for him to learn the modern language. To add to that, there were times where he would doze off suddenly and wake up hours or days later, nauseated and dizzy, unable to correctly piece together what was happening or what he was saying.

To be sure, the only place I could head to is Massilia, if it is still called that... and if it is still there. That sanctuary was hidden in the hills overlooking the sea and the whole of the Massilian Urbis. I hope it's still there; it would be nice to have some help of others from the order instead of having to rely on swindling poor fools.

He laughed to himself and staggered up. It was time to sleep and tomorrow would bring him within three days of Massilia. Picking up his lance, he scattered the fire and then carefully gathered the stones he kept at its base and buried them under the spot where he prepared his bed. As he lay down, he could feel the warmth seeping up into his back. He grinned; it was as comfortable as anything he could have hoped for in the wild.

*****

The rising moon shone brightly across the landscape, casting distorted shadows where the forests and looming Alps met long stretches of plains. There were few nocturnal creatures about, but slowly over a stretch of land came two wondering shapes. It was Meliore leading Corbella straight for Corlieu's encampment. They approached it from atop a ledge and inched their way to the edge until they were looking down upon Corlieu's sleeping form.

"There he is," whispered Meliore, peering over the cliff to the ground below. "I can't believe that he's here, we barely have been riding! He must have not expected much from us if he only went this far."

Corbella shook her head before realizing that Meliore wasn't looking.

"I don't care, that swindler brought us out here and we are going to make him pay for what he did."

Meliore jumped up, a look of wild glee on her face. In her excitement, some of the dirt scattered off the edge of the cliff, raining on the ground below.

"Cut it out," whispered Corbella sharply. *"Don't you dare wake him up now that we're so close! We had to watch forever to make sure it was him and he was alone."*

As she said that, a large rock slid right in front of Meliore, who was too preoccupied to notice. Corbella gasped and made a leap for it, crashing into Meliore who shrieked and flailed wildly and struck her clear across the shoulder, knocking Corbella off the side of the cliff.

"CURSE YOU MELIORE!" yelled Corbella as she rolled over the edge. The only thing she remembered was sky–ground–sky–ground–pain. Luckily it was not a far drop, but it went straight down onto Corlieu's camp.

"Corbella, are you okay?!" came Meliore, scrambling down the side and running over.

Corbella was too angry to do anything. The pain was surprisingly mild, but her back ached as she reached up and grabbed Meliore by the shirt. Taken aback by her cousin's anger, Meliore turned to try and get away, but it was too late. She was too close and Corbella already had a firm grip on her.

"I can't believe you just did that, you could have killed me!"

"I didn't mean to, it just happened," Meliore said, trying to scramble away. "Why did you lunge at me like that anyways?"

"A rock was rolling right over the edge next to you. I didn't want it to wake... wait, where is Corlieu?"

Meliore peered down without so much as moving a muscle. Corbella followed her eyes, feeling her muscles tighten and her hairs stand on edge. Somehow, impossibly, she had landed right upon Corlieu. Even more astonishing than that, he hadn't even moved.

"What the heck?" Corbella said, forgetting all of her indignation. "How can he still be asleep?"

"Maybe you killed him?" said Meliore, moving away and crouching down, close to his face.

"He's breathing… he's not dead," she paused, hovering over him for a little while. After a moment she sat up, screwed up her face and then moved her ear to his mouth.

"I can hardly believe it," she said, finally sitting up. "He's asleep!"

"How could he be asleep still?" asked Corbella. "I landed on him!"

"Don't look at me, I thought he was dearly departed after that. I've never heard of anyone sleeping this hard, do you think he had too much to drink?"

"Drink doesn't do this," said Corbella. "Besides, you would have this horrible odor. Something like old salted pork and feet."

Corbella just sat dumbfounded a moment, she didn't know what to do. They finally captured Corlieu and it was without a fight or anything. All their concern about him was pointless because here he was as helpless as a baby.

"Break out the rope," said Corbella. "It's time to tie this guy up."

They sat facing a still sleeping Corlieu. Neither Meliore or Corbella knew how to bind a person so they hastily went to work wrapping him in as much spare rope as they could manage. By the time they were finished, the effect looked similar to entrapping him in a ball of string and Corbella was certain it would do the trick.

Gradually, he began to shift and mutter in his sleep. As morning came, he suddenly rocked his head back and opened his eyes. He looked around in complete confusion, not even noticing the girls as they sat attentively now, waiting for him to notice them. When he didn't, Corbella coughed and spoke.

"Well it's about time that you woke up, I thought you were going to sleep forever."

He swiveled his head in a curious fashion and stared at her for a moment.

"Who are you?" he asked.

"You do not recognize us?" said Meliore, sounding shocked and looking hesitantly at Corbella.

"If I could see then 1 wouldn't be asking would I?" came his irritated tone. "What has happened, I cannot move."

"Now, that's not a nice tone to take towards us," said Corbella. "It's hard to believe that you'd forget us so soon after running out with all our money."

"Oh, it's you two girls," he finally said.

"Most certainly yes," said Corbella. "If you don't want us to kill you now, you'll tell us what you did with the money you took!

Corbella did her best to sound mean and threatening. Meliore certainly recoiled to one side at her cousin's tone, but Corlieu merely laughed. He must know as she did that it was a hollow threat. There would be no way she could actually bring herself to kill anyone and somehow it showed in her tone.

"This is certainly great fortune," he said. "You do realize that most of the money on the table was not rightfully yours since we were in the middle of a set of wagers. Who are you to call me such names when it was clear that you would have made off with it all yourselves."

"That's beside the point," said Corbella. "I was merely trying to make sure you did not flee with it!"

"If you can barely convince yourself of that, then that reason will hardly work on anyone else" said Corlieu with smirk. "Then what are you going to do afterwards? Maybe I'll be on your tracks, looking to get my revenge. There's no use heading back to Genoa for you two. Faces and mannerisms as orderly and well kept at yours mean you two were from well to do families…"

Corbella felt her insides tighten a little bit at these words. Something of their tension must have shown in one of their faces because Corlieu merely grinned and kept on speaking.

"I see I am close to the mark. Two runaways from rich families, my I wonder how big of a reward there is for you two renegades of Genoa. Especially after the show you orchestrated Ms. Corbella."

"*SILENCE!*" Corbella shouted. "I will not listen to these faulty stories. We've done nothing wrong and simply believe in good etiquette."

At this Corlieu laughed hard and for a while the only words he would say were "good etiquette? You have to be jesting!" Finally he caught his breath and continued on.

"If you're going to survive without your family's protection, you're going to need a better story than that. Also Ms. Meliore, I understand you have something that belongs to me. Two things, two very ornate and gorgeous pieces that were on the table that were rightfully mine."

She gasped and her hand twitched to her pocket.

"We don't have anything," cut in Corbella impatiently. "That's the whole reason we came after you, to get what's rightfully ours back. We're not thieves and never intended to be."

"You're off to a good start learning," Corlieu said.

"I've had enough of this. Meliore, let's go!"

"And you're going to leave me?"

Corbella simply nodded.

"But, wait a minute. It's not right to just abandon someone in the wild."

"You dumb clod! If it wasn't for you, we wouldn't be out here in the first place. We would both be in our room, comfortable and asleep by now instead of out here in the cold. You get whatever's coming to you."

Corlieu began to fight and thrash around.

"*GET ME OUT OF HERE, CUT ME LOOSE!*"

His yelling was in vain however because Corbella and Meliore had walked out of sight. Dawn was approaching and Meliore wanted to get to Marseilles as soon as was possible. It was at the last moment that Corbella decided to take

Corlieu's horse. Even though Meliore told her she had no reservations against continuing to Marseilles riding double, Corbella had insisted on taking Corlieu's horse. She argued that they couldn't leave his horse there so he could soon follow after them. Together, they packed away some things including the remaining money they plundered from Corlieu's bags and set off.

Chapter 7

The morning sun breached the horizon and started its climb up to the heavens. The world was quiet, disturbed only by the rustle of animals and the crack of foliage under hoof.

Meliore and Corbella came riding over the top of a hill and along a path hedging along a stretch of forest. Meliore sat peacefully atop her horse Stocatta, occasionally looking over the an increasingly frustrated Corbella. Corlieu's horse was a type and temperament they had never encountered before. It was incredibly hostile and had a habit of putting its head down and pulling on the reins when she wasn't paying attention before bolting off suddenly and without provocation. It also seemed to use any excuse as a reason to rapidly shy away and it nearly managed to dismount Corbella twice.

"Do you think he'll escape?" asked Meliore.

"Who, this little beast?" asked Corbella as the horse threw a kick.

"No, I mean Corlieu. We're in a lot of trouble if he does."

"I don't think it's his fate to die all tied up in the woods."

"But then," stammered Meliore, "aren't you worried that he'll want revenge? He nicely ripped us off in Genoa, but this time around he might do worse."

"Who's to tell? I doubt he'll be that ill disposed towards us. He was the one who ripped us off first after all, so the blame for starting all this was with him. All the same, be careful. The sooner we get to Marseilles, the better."

Meliore let out a long sigh and stood up, pushing her weight into her stirrups and stretching a moment with a gigantic yawn. She exclaimed a moment and sat down hurriedly.

"I've forgotten but you have never been to Marseilles. I still don't know why I had the chance for traveling but your father never wanted to take you. You'll see soon enough however, it is an amazing place. The beautiful buildings, the people and the great food...."

"Meliore, that was then with your family," said Corbella, cutting into Meliore's rambling. "This is now and we're without the privilege you had. We'll hardly see much of the city's good side in our predicament."

"I don't understand Corbella!" said Meliore after a moment. "Here we are having just gotten our revenge on Corlieu, we're heading to a beautiful city and you cannot allow yourself to relax and enjoy this moment like I am. It is a burden on my mood."

"It's easy for you to feel happy, you're dwelling on memories of luxury. I don't have such memories and all I can think about is what we can do to survive. Corlieu was right, he did spend most of the money. We'll have to think of something quickly when we arrive."

Meliore rode quietly for a while. She opened her mouth a few times, but encouraging words did not come to her so she just fell in to a shallow gloom while occasionally goading the horse into a trot up inclines and glancing over to ensure Corbella and her mean horse were okay. More valleys and tall grass surrounded by woods littered the path while the hills to the north gave way to low, green mountains. Behind these, there were greater mountains, gray and cradling some vestiges of snow.

The afternoon wore on into evening and still the landscape looked the same. Meliore and Corbella talked sparingly, trying to plan what their next actions should be. They agreed that they should stop on the outskirts of town and change back into their male personas. Meliore's mood was further depressed when Corbella mentioned that they would probably have to sell the two horses. It made sense and she had realized this herself during the day's travel. Keeping a horse was an expense and commitment she could not afford anymore, but she still vainly clung to the hope that she could find a way to keep Stocatta.

"Meliore, do you see that?" said Corbella suddenly, bringing the horse to a stop and pointing off in the distance.

Meliore had been hanging her head. A bout of drowsiness had such a considerable grip on her that Corbella had to slap her across the back. She popped up, looking around suddenly before she caught sight of what Corbella was pointing towards.

The valley around them turned red as the sun began to set. A large cloud, increasingly menacing, loomed in front of them. Meliore also noticed that there were tiny wisps floating gently from the sky. As they continued on, the flakes became more numerous. She waited patiently with her palm upturned and managed to catch one. The little chip was gray and black, easily turning into powder in her hand.

"They're ashes," said Meliore after a little bit of thought. "Oh no....they're in the direction of Marseilles too."

Corbella didn't say anything and only moved her horse into a trot. Corbella followed up behind and they made their way quickly up the last hill and stopped short. Meliore looked and was stunned into silence.

Below them, they saw a city. Its edges spread out for a distance along the coast in a great triangular shape. The large harbor was shielded from the sea by a cluster of islands and enclosed by the city on one side and an outcropping of hills on the other.

It must have once been beautiful.

Slowly, the horse picked its way through the ruins of Marseilles. Corbella's horse seemed to feel the magnitude of the disaster around them and was obedient for the first time that day. They walked them through the ruins, picking a way through the broken streets and smoldering wreckage.

Every building was blackened and hanging in ruins. The remaining fires, consuming what was left of the city, spat up great clouds of smoke and flashing red embers. It was as close to a vision of hell as Meliore could ever imagine. Everything she knew and cared about in that city was destroyed, consumed in fire and twisted into hideous shapes. Never before had she felt so depressed.

"What happened here?" asked Corbella, looking around as the horse walked slowly through the littered streets.

Meliore was unable to respond. She didn't know how to respond. Who could have devastated this city? It was beyond her to imagine what kind of awesome power could have done such a thing.

"Where are the people?" said Corbella. "There are not even any dead upon the ground. Have you noticed?"

It took Meliore by surprise that she didn't realize this at first. Despite all the destruction, there wasn't anything alive or dead. Everybody had simply vanished and left everything to burn.

"It's getting late; the sun will go down in a little. We should find somewhere to camp," Corbella said, turning around and looking at Meliore. "You okay?"

Meliore opened her mouth to say something again, but couldn't find words.

She looked at Corbella and just shrugged before turning her head and looking around her again.

Night had now crept on the ruins of Marseilles, turning the blackened city into a collection of glowing debris. All night, Meliore kept tossing and turning, unable to sufficiently relax and occasionally went to lean on Stocatta, feeling her horses' calming breath before trying to return to sleep. She had recovered from the shock just enough to help Corbella set up a shelter for their horses earlier and look for supplies, but their search was in vain. There was little of use which escaped the fire and every building they had come across had been torn apart. They settled for making a spot where a section of wall still stood supported by a crumpled roof and enclosed within a circle of debris. The ground was covered in stone with broken edges, making it difficult to find a comfortable place to sleep.

Meliore rose from her blankets and walked out again, passing by Corbella who laid motionless. She too had arisen a few times during the night, but merely sat wordlessly. It was comfortable outside, not nearly as windy as Genoa and the sound of the waves on the beach was vaguely soothing, but it was not enough.

They were camping on a street Meliore remembered. Every corner harbored some familiar memory when she was younger and life was easier. Everything was provided for her: food, shelter, comfort and entertainment. It was such a lovely time that now could never be again. The brief moment she got to spend lounging around with Corbella after running away was the closest she had ever gotten to that childlike, carefree lifestyle. Corlieu had come and forced them into a ceaseless journey from one hovel to another. Her memories of her carefree life like her recollections of Marseilles, were just that: memories and nothing else. She felt the pangs of home return to her again and she went over to Stocatta, running her hand across his side and hearing his reassuring nicker before resting her head on his flank.

Would you go back home? You already promised to stick with Corbella but given your own choice without her to consider, would you? This life on your own is going poorly and unless you think of something in the next two days, the food is going to run out. Is it even possible to make it back if we wanted?

Again, Meliore shook her head and sighed. Their supplies would not last a trip back to Genoa and if Alessandro was any indication of anything, their punishments would be severe.

Stocatta suddenly picked up his head, ears straight and glanced around fully awake. Meliore could feel his body tense and she ran her hand across his neck and looked around, frightened and suddenly alert.

What was that? I thought I heard something off in the distance...

She strained her ears, trying to slow her beating heart so she could hear whatever was out there in the darkness.

There it is again, is that...whinnying?

With a gasp, she suddenly remembered that she didn't check on the other horse. Meliore sprinted back to the spot where they tied the horse up.

He was gone.

"CORBELLA! WAKE UP! YOUR HORSE IS GONE!" she yelled.

Corbella flew up out of bed, peddling her feet in the air for a second or two before arising and running over to Meliore.

"DON'T YELL! WHAT'S GOING ON?"

"The horse," said Meliore. "Corlieu's horse is gone and I thought I heard it out in the distance."

This time, clear and audible, they both heard a whinny. It was close this time, sounding as though it was within the burnt city.

"C'mon," said Corbella getting up quickly and walking out into the street. "As much of a pain as that horse is, we'll need him too. When morning comes, we'll have to get away forthwith and I'm sure it's going to be a long way to the next town."

"Where to next?" asked Meliore doubtfully. "I remember the only other city nearby is far off along the coast."

Corbella opened her mouth and closed it again.

"I haven't a clue but we'll worry about that later. Is Stocatta okay at least?"

Meliore nodded and Corbella let out an audible sigh.

"Thank the heavens," she said.

It was slow going. Despite the glow from the dying embers of the fires, it was still dark out. The moon was a faint sliver and offered scarce additional light. It seemed as though Meliore tripped over every broken fragment and outcropping along their way. Aside from their breathing and Corbella's occasional cursing, there were no other noises.

"Wait," whispered Meliore, grabbing ahold of Corbella and hunkering down. *"What's that over there? Something is moving…"*

They crouched down and remained motionless for a moment. Ahead, there was a dark shape in the street, crawling to the wreckage of a building. It made soft noises, barely audible.

"I can't tell what that is from here," Corbella whispered. *"I need to get closer."*

Meliore took a deep breath and followed after her cousin. They walked along the side of the street behind the crawling thing and closed in on it slowly. At a distance of twenty feet, they stopped. Whatever the thing was had stopped moving and swung around, propped up by an arm.

"Who's there?" came a man's voice. "I'm armed so don't be foolish."

The suddenness of the voice came as a shock to Meliore. Its deep, serious tone made her jump and she forgot her prudence for the moment.

"Please, um…sir. We're not going to hurt you," she said.

The man froze in place for a few moments. Meliore was beginning to wonder if she said anything wrong and if he was going to do anything to them. Suddenly, he laughed. It was a deep throaty laugh that gargled a little at the end.

"Girls? Why in heaven's name are there girls in a place like this? Of all unexpected things to come across in a ruined city, but this is far more fortunate than a pair of thieves or brigands."

"And how do you know we're not still?" asked Corbella. Her voice was as stern as she could make it, but it was not stern enough apparently because the man laughed again.

"You don't sound like it. Your friend gave you both away so even in my condition I know I hardly need to worry. I don't know what could have brought you out here, or what you did to escape the destruction of this place, but it's okay by me."

He collapsed back on the floor with a grunt and Meliore followed Corbella closer to his side. They could see he was injured. His clothes were dark and matted in several places from near the neck down to his calves. His breathing was heavy and his eyes were closed.

"Water…or beer. Wine or something! Is there anything to drink 'twixt you two…" was all that he said.

"Wait," said Corbella, getting up and running off. "I'll get my water. Stay with him!"

Meliore sat there, next to the man. His breathing had gotten heavier and was occasionally punctuated by gasps. With nothing better to do, she started trying to tend to his wounds but the man waved her off.

"I'm fear I'm dying," he said. "It's useless trying to help me. You'll just make it hurt more."

He lay there, taking big mouthfuls of air and looking at Meliore. She started to feel agitated under his unceasing stare.

Where is Corbella? I hope she's alright.

The man coughed again, sending a trail of blood coming down the sides of his mouth.

"Sorry, I didn't mean to stare. It's just, you remind me of one of my daughters. It's a cruel life that robs me of the chance to ever see her again."

He propped himself up, cringing with the effort.

"Save your strength," Meliore said, taking a hold of him awkwardly and trying to decide whether to help him sit up or lay back down.

"C'mere," he whispered. "You need to know something before I expire. I don't trust that other fellow but he's gone now. He has the look of a scoundrel but you girls need to know something…"

******

Corbella was running back from her encampment. The uneven ground and scattered timbers made it extremely difficult to run, but she kept it up somehow without completely falling down.

Where are they? They should be somewhere down by this place…

As she spun around, she saw that they moved over a little, into the shadows of a building. Corbella ran up and she could see Meliore crouching right next to the man. She looked as though she was holding him in her arms and her faint voice murmured over the wind.

"MELIORE!" she yelled, running over. "What are you doing, don't get that close to him!"

Meliore didn't say anything or even acknowledge that Corbella was there. Her head was downcast, facing the man who was wordlessly lying in her arms.

"It's…it's okay Corbella," she said. "He's dead, there's nothing to worry about."

Corbella stared down at the man, unable to do anything except stand there agape.

"Have you ever seen anyone die?" asked Meliore, breaking a minute's worth of silence and looking up.

"No, I never. Well never live…" she stammered, struck by the odd tone in Meliore's voice.

Meliore looked back down, leaving Corbella standing uncomfortably. She leaned from side to side, making a few attempts to say or do something. Nothing seemed appropriate however and it was sometime before Meliore moved.

"We should go," Meliore said, lowering the man gently to the ground. "I'm sorry, didn't know what came over me. Just have never seen anyone die in front of me before. We need to go, we can't stay here. There's someone else around here, someone that's not to be trus…"

Corbella heard the sounds of hooves close by, cantering up the street. She wheeled around, ready to sprint for a hiding spot but it was too late. They spent too much time and even in the shadows, they were in the relative open. In a few seconds, the stranger was upon them.

The rider came, dismounted and lead his horse up before stopping some ways away staring at them. Corbella rose slowly, unsure of what to make of him and backing up nearby Meliore. She cursed quietly under her breath for letting Meliore delay them for so long. Now here they were, caught and defenseless.

The rider let out a cry of frustration.

"I KNEW IT! I JUST KNEW YOU TWO WOULD BE HERE!" he said.

Corbella cocked her head. She recognized that voice.

"Corlieu?" she said hesitantly.

"YES, IT'S ME CURSE IT ALL!" he said, sliding off the side of the horse and walking over to the man. "Is he still alive?"

"No," said Meliore. "He died only a short time ago."

Corlieu came up and crouched next to him. After a moment, he let out a long sigh, crossed his arm over his chest a moment and stood back up.

"He is a brigand, I ran into him as he was hobbling severely injured into the ruins here. I hoped he could tell about what happened here and if he saw any signs of you two. He told me little, almost violently resisted any help I offered and ran this way."

"So you heard your horse and went to go get him?" Corbella asked.

"Exactly, it was a choice between following this hostile fellow or getting my horse back. I don't know what you two have been up to, but you must have let him run wild a lot. It took much longer to catch him than usual. I thought at first he dumped one of you and ran off on his own, but then I got this bad feeling that you were both here."

Corbella backed towards his horse a few steps. As Corlieu talked, she inched a few more steps towards his horse. There was a large sword strapped to the saddlebags and she slowly pulled it out. She didn't trust Corlieu and though the sword was extremely heavy, it was at least something she could bludgeon with.

"Sure enough," continued Corlieu, looking up and disregarding the fact that she was holding his sword, "I came over here as fast as I could and there you two were, huddled over his body. Was he alive earlier?"

Corbella nodded. Corlieu looked shocked for a moment and came rushing over.

"Did he say anything to you?!?" he said, flailing his hands in eagerness.

Meliore coughed and they both turned to look at her curiously. A faint smile crawled across her lips.

"He said you were here and....some other things."

Corlieu moved crossed the ground to her, opening and closing his mouth. His hands grasped the open air in frustration. Meliore stood there, unintimidated by him and he finally sighed again, throwing up his hands and turning around.

"You have some nerve, girl. What do you plan on doing with that information anyways?"

"I suppose I will just have to keep it to myself and use it as I see fit."

"Don't be foolish," said Corlieu. "I will have to know, whatever he was after is probably responsible for all of this," he said, holding his hands out and motioning around them. "Can't you see that there is something greater at work here? I doubt this was caused by something as simple as an accidental fire."

"There were enough things he said that I could understand," Meliore said. "He didn't know what burnt down this city, it was alive and thriving last time he saw it."

Corlieu looked defeated for a moment. He took a deep breath and looked from one girl to the other.

"Okay then, so what is that you want?"

"You want whatever that brigand was chasing, right?" asked Meliore. "He told me where he was going, what it was and where exactly it is kept. You can help us get this....um, treasure and escape."

"Hold on," said Corbella, letting the sword fall and grabbing a hold of Meliore. "What are you doing?!? He already ripped us off before and now you want to make him our partner?"

"Did you not say a day ago that he wouldn't hurt us?"

"This is different!" said Corbella. "While I don't believe he'll skewer us like a pair of rodents, I think not that he'll be our faithful companion."

"I think it'll be okay," said Meliore. "We have information he'll need, so he can't do anything to us. If he wants this treasure, he'll have to behave."

"And what keeps him from kidnapping me and forcing the information out of you or something?" Corbella protested.

Meliore looked down and furrowed her eyebrows. It was obvious that this had not occurred to her and she was suddenly in doubt. Finally, she shrugged and looked over at Corlieu, who was impatiently waiting for them.

"I don't think we have much of a choice," she finally said in a whisper. "It's not like we can lose him, not yet at least. Plus he might know how to go about doing this. We have to find a castle, but I have never heard of it before and there's no way we could escape on our own."

"Finished, little ladies?" asked Corlieu.

Corbella turned around, irritated at his choice of words and heaved the sword back up.

"Alright," said Corbella. "We don't have much of a choice at the moment. I don't like it, but for now we've got ourselves a deal."

Corlieu smiled and walked over. He looked amused by their arguments for and against him.

"Good," he said. "You two will never make it in the wild country alone." He stopped and glanced sidelong at Corbella. His eyes drifted down to his sword at her side. "Um...what were you planning on doing with that? You can hardly lift it."

Blood rushed to Corbella's cheeks and she found herself stammer with indignation. Corlieu just laughed and walked over to the horses and rummaged through his gear. While he was doing that, Meliore came up next to Corbella.

"You know, he's right," she said. "You really never would be able to lift that thing long enough to do anything with it."

"And if I could, I'd hack your tongue off first," she said through her clenched teeth.

"One last thing," Corlieu said, coming over and grabbing his sword out of Corbella's hands. "It might interest you two to know how I escaped."

A curious gleam came across his eyes as he looked at them both.

"So I was correct and you two are the runaway brides. You know, Genoa and

Venice are at war thanks to you two?"

"How do you know about that?" Corbella stammered in shock. Again, her cheeks flushed in embarrassment and fury. "I'm not a runaway bride, I never agreed to anything!"

"You don't have to in these days," Corlieu said. "Your agreement was unnecessary, but your disappearance was quite devastating."

"So how do you know about us?" asked Meliore sternly.

"There's someone named Alessandro looking for you both. I think you might know who he is, right Meliore?"

There was a long pause.

"He...is? No...he can't be..." Meliore said, backing away and stumbling over some rubble. "My brother, he can't be chasing after us."

"Yes, he is. He found me when I was still tied up and set me free if I'd help him find you."

Corbella stiffened. She had never anticipated that anyone would follow after them outside of Genoa. What would happen if they were caught? She couldn't imagine what her family would do to her, especially if the war that Corlieu mentioned was true. Her temper flared when Corlieu gave a sudden snort of laughter.

"It's lucky he didn't recognize me from earlier, he might have just stuck me like a pig and left me there. As it was, they didn't and I told Alessandro's little hunting party that you were heading up to Lyon and were short on supplies when you two ran across me in my sleep."

"And he believed that?" asked Meliore. "Why didn't you lead him here? After all, I wouldn't have been surprised since you would be looking for some way to get back at us."

Corlieu nodded and raised a hand.

"I don't like your brother. The first instant I saw him and the more time I spent in his company, the less I liked him. I wouldn't want to travel with these guys either. Your brother seems like a real clumsy savage and I'll guess that you two were not close. He'll be lucky if someone doesn't try to rob him with the way he blunders about, yelling at all hours and making a scene. But now that we're both out here and going after this treasure, I'll say that we'll be even in a little bit anyways."

Corbella was still uncertain. Corlieu seemed very crafty and she didn't like the thought of having to travel with him, especially into the wilderness. Corlieu seemed to read some of her thoughts and he came over to her.

"Look," he said, holding up his hands and pointing off into the distance. "I don't know what luck you had getting here, but it won't last long in the wilderness. There are thieves, animals and do you even know where you're going?

Corbella shook her head slowly, keeping Corlieu at a distance.

"I can help you make it, we could find out where this treasure is and live the good life off our riches. As long as there's something in it for me, then we have a deal."

"You told us we'd have to watch out for crooks out there, right? Well aren't you the guy who started this whole problem by ripping us off in the first place?"

"Pardon, but I was seriously desperate," he said as a smirked crossed his lips. "Besides, you lunged at the money just the same as I did. I hardly think I'm to blame if we had the same thoughts but I just happened to get it. I suppose we should have stopped in the burning building and pieced it out nice and properly, right?"

"Very well," said Corbella turning to Meliore. "I still don't quite trust you but I'd say that I'm convinced enough to go along with this."

"Corbella and Meliore at your service," Meliore said, extending her hand.

"Corlieu at yours, my ladies," he said, meeting her hand and shaking it.

Chapter 8

Corlieu lay wrapped in his heavy clothes and hunkered down in the company of a large tree that jutted out of a small dell. It was not the best shelter, but it helped to deflect the wind so that he was amazingly snug throughout the night. He peeked up, over the flap of cloth he wrapped over his face.

The dark frame of the forest and low hills were illuminated by the pale orange of the rising sun. A very dreary weight hung on his every limb and the chilly morning bit at his exposed face. As much as he would have liked to continue his sleep, he knew that they needed to get moving.

Blast that Meliore, what could this ever so important treasure be? If she just told me a little more, I could know what's afoot. Clearly the army that ransacked Marseilles thought it was important enough.

Corlieu stood up and stretched before grabbing a biscuit and sitting down to think. It felt good to move again after spending most of the night thinking about their situation. Aside from this great treasure, he was thinking about what had run through and burnt Marseilles. Though the brigand turned downright hostile when the talk turned to the treasure he was pursuing, he did tell Corlieu about what he had been through to suffice.

We tracked this caravan ever since it left Marseilles. Whate'er it was had been locked away in a cart. With a guard that large, something valuable was being transported. Our ambush was poorly timed, reinforcements came down the road and surrounded us. When it was hopeless, we turned to escape. I know not how but I escaped with many wounds.

A flutter of birds vacating a nearby tree broke Corlieu's thoughts. After watching them fly off for a moment, he sat down and rummaged through his bag for some biscuits before remembering the remainder of the guard's story.

When night fell, I made my way to Marseilles hoping to find help. There was a plume of smoke spreading over the city and the glow of great fires. Whatever army did this came swiftly past in the night pursuing the caravan. I could do nothing but cower in a bush I threw myself into. They had human shapes that were distorted and vaguely outlined as though they were made out of smoke. I could feel the tramp of feet and hear the clatter of their arms, but their torchlights shone through them. It reminded me of seeing thousands of shapes through a murky pond. When they passed and I reached the city, I found it this way. Burnt and abandoned...

A rustling noise broke his concentration and he stuffed the remainder of his biscuit in his mouth and walked up the dell to the girls' encampment. As the morning sun broke upon their encampment, he nearly choked at what he saw.

There was no semblance of order other than vague areas where equipment had been discarded in the night. Clothes hung on bushes and trees, food was scattered and it looked as though some of it had been rummaged through and eaten by nocturnal wildlife. The fire from the previous night had been untended and had consumed a nearby bush at some point in the night. Corlieu couldn't believe it and he had to strain to keep from yelling.

"WAKE UP!" he shouted after a second of trying to figure out what to do. *"TIME TO GET UP AND CLEAN THIS MESS OF YOURS."*

Meliore opened her eye and looked around. She was laying, half smashed against Corbella and had in the night, rolled over her and sprawled out. It was a small wonder how she managed to stay warm in the night. She groaned and stretched before sitting straight up and looking around.

"What's for breakfast?" she asked, looking at Corlieu. He was taken aback. He bit back a sharp retort and had to remind himself that they probably had never camped outdoors.

"Don't look at me like that, your breakfast is whatever's left around that hasn't already been eaten."

She gazed left and right, seeming not to comprehend what he was talking about until her eyes centered on a trail of half–eaten food.

"CORBELLA! WAKE UP, YOU DIDN'T PUT THE FOOD AWAY!"

Corbella rolled over and squinted at both of them.

"Do you not remember? I told you to when I was going to sleep."

"Most certainly not! You said you were going to put everything away before going to sleep."

"That hardly even sounds like something I'd say!"

They bickered back and forth a few moments more. Throughout this, Corlieu silently looked from one to the other before sighing and turning back to his encampment. He wondered how long he would survive with these two and if there was any chance he could figure out what to do without Meliore's help.

It didn't take him long to pack all his gear, grab a little bit more food and situate himself. The girls took his advice the previous night and they all left the ruins, heading northwards until Corlieu came upon a spot that looked suitable.

Before they went to sleep, he lit a fire and they were able to warm themselves a moment. He told them a little about what he knew, but it was hard for him to keep his concentration. In the light of the campfire, he could see the gleam of two small, square pieces in Meliore's hand. He was astounded to realize that she forgot they were his and was lackadaisically rolling them around from one hand to the other as she talked. He retired first, finding a comfortable spot and spent the rest of his night puzzling over why two pieces of his precious dice seemed to be more favorable towards her than him. His dice never betrayed him, and yet that night those two favored her as much as the rest of the set did with him.

Corlieu stood up, donning his bag and taking one more glance to make sure he wasn't forgetting anything. It was then that he noticed that the girls had stopped arguing and everything was once again quiet. He hurried over, wondering what could have happened now.

Their encampment was empty. He looked from one side to the other, again slightly astonished. All their clothes were gone, the litter on the floor had disappeared as well and the ashes from the fire were covered and disguised. Corlieu shook his head and looked around, not knowing where they could have gone off to, doubtful that they were responsible enough to have cleaned everything up themselves so quickly, but quite sure that they wouldn't have abandoned him.

"Did someone notice us and come by when I wasn't paying attention?"

He heard voices coming from a little ways off and hurried over. He gripped his sword uncertainly and tried to determine what was going on from the tone of their voices. Silently, looking from side to side, he crept over towards a stream where he heard splashing.

"Oh no…"

Corlieu waited at some distance, feeling slightly irritated. They were bathing of all things as though they were in the privacy and security of their own home. Unsure of what to do, he sat down and waited against a tree. Finally Corbella came walking past and running a brush through her hair followed by Meliore who was clutching for the comb. They were dry, dressed and smelled of flowers and perfumes of some sort. Resting his head in his hands and covering his eyes, Corlieu coughed and hear a muffled yelp.

"WERE YOU…SPYING ON US?" asked Corbella angrily.

"Not to worry I had not a glance. Are you two decent now? Why on earth were you bathing? Can you not realize the risk involved?"

"We checked, nobody was around," she said. "Besides, we were dirty."

"How dirty could you possibly have been? You couldn't have bathed more than two days ago by my guess."

"Isn't that long enough?" Meliore said.

"No, it is not. You need to never do that again while we're out here."

"Why? You can't tell us what to do!" they both said in unison.

Corlieu looked up, feeling his blood pressure rise slightly.

"I need to keep you two alive," said Corlieu. "Only the sons and daughters of rich families bathe with that kind of frequency. The richer ones…" he continued, smelling the air deeply and wrinkling his nose," …also wear perfumes. If anyone with a mind for ransom comes by while you smell like that, then you're done for."

Both girls stammered and looked at each other. It was clear to Corlieu that those things had never crossed their minds before.

"Don't worry about it now, the damage is done and I expected nobody around anyways," Corlieu said getting to his feet and hoisting his bag. "We ought to get moving, but first you can't leave your hair out like that and I must insist that you continue dressing up as men."

Once again, he could see the girls get ready to launch a fresh round of complaints, but Corlieu could stand little more that morning.

"ENOUGH!" he shouted. "Just trust me on this. People will think twice about attacking three men in the wild, even if they do smell a little questionable; but one man and two girls?"

With no verbal argument but a lot of grumbling, they subjected themselves to whatever recommendations he gave them, including taking some of his dirtier clothing to help disguise themselves and stuffing all of their hair underneath their hats like they did in Genoa.

"I'd prefer if you just cut your hair off completely," said Corlieu, helping Meliore stuff hers in her hat.

"DON'T YOU EVEN THINK ABOUT IT CORLIEU!" she shouted. "I'll wear my hat day and night if I have to, but you're not touching the hair."

The remainder of that day was spent pursuing the army. As large a force as it must have been to decimate Marseilles so thoroughly, it left no prints. The dirt along the way was fresh and unsoiled, making the footing comfortable for their horses to trot along. However, the trees were burnt and slashed, bushes were uprooted, and rocks were shattered and broken. The world around was shadowed in a gleam of red that grew ever stronger the further north they went.

Though much of their ride was spent in silence, Corlieu still managed to find himself exasperated by the girls. His suspicions that they had never so much as stepped out into the wild were more correct than he even feared. There was a constant stream of complaints concerning the various problems they were having with their horse, the insects, the lack of breaks, the heat that day and the general unpleasantness of the decimation they were following. He was constantly reminding himself to watch his temper.

"HOLD ON, WAIT A SECOND!" came a voice from behind him.

"What is it now?" he asked, taking a deep breath and turning around.

"Just want to take a break for a second," Corbella said, sliding off one side of her horse pulling out a brush and running it through her hair.

"Did you really have to stop and get off your horse to do that? We're wasting…," Corlieu started before being interrupted.

"May I have that after you're done with it?" asked Meliore, leaning over the horse and reaching out.

"I TOLD YOU NO! WHAT HAPPENED TO YOURS?" Corbella said recoiling.

"It broke and it was my only one. C'mon, just for a minute or so."

They argued back and forth for a moment, but their dispute was broken when Corlieu came between them and plucked the brush out of Corbella's hand. He walking to one side of the route they had been following and threw it sidelong into the bushes a good deal away.

"There," he said, storming back over to his horse and ground mounting. "Dispute settled, let's get on again."

"Why did you do that?" asked Corbella angrily.

"Men out in the wild don't comb their hair," he said, shaking his unkempt locks. "Remember what I told you, you need to pass as boys and you're doing a miserable job at that."

"Who made you the leader?" asked a haughty Corbella.

"Nobody did, but if you want to survive out here where there is no law, comfort or servants waiting on you, you'll need to listen to me. I was hoping to get to our destination before the army did, but at our pace we'll be lucky to make it at all."

"What do you mean," asked Corbella, standing up and walking towards Corlieu. "You said that the passage of this army probably either killed or drove off everyone for a good distance around us?"

"Yes, that's true if we're close behind it or even remotely near it. By my estimate, we're a little over half the needed distance and the army should already be there. We are relatively safe from them. If there is a treasure that's attracting a force *THAT* great, then you can be certain that any second class gutter thieves will be thinking about taking a chance at it after some time has passed."

"You mean thieves like us, eh?" said Meliore.

Corlieu snorted.

"You two are hardly worth the name. Luck has more to do with any thieving involving you two rather than skill."

Meliore just sat and glared while Corbella paced about.

"Alright, so we might be more lucky than anything else," Corbella said after a moment. "No, as much as I'd hate to admit it, he's right Meliore. What are we supposed to do about it though? We don't know anything about being out here, or fighting or treasure hunting. We were born to rich trading families as you said and the most adventure we had come from occasionally riding horses like this one from the livery barn."

Corlieu was thrown a little off guard by her admission. Corbella to him seemed to be the most headstrong and the least likely to cave in to anything, whether it made sense or not.

"If you're willing to learn, I'll teach you what I know to survive out here," he said. "The most useful thing you can do at the moment is learn to fight. Do you have a weapon?"

The girls looked at each other and simultaneously held up their fists. Corlieu laughed and drew his massive sword.

"Against something like this, your fists have little chance unless you know exactly what you're doing and I don't." He swung the sword from side to side, it whistled through the air as he twirled it effortlessly around his body. He walked over to a branch cut from a nearby tree and went to work, cutting pieces and whittling extra limbs off before returning to the girls.

"This isn't the best by a long shot, but it'll do the job for now better than anything," he said, giving them each a crooked four foot stick each and keeping one for himself.

"Now, hold it up like so," he said, holding up the branch he fashioned for himself. Corbella readily obeyed. Meliore, who was a little hesitant, suffered the first hit.

TWACK!

She yelped in shock as Corlieu struck her on the shoulder. He was sure that it was light enough to only sting, but even still he could see the outline of a red mark.

"That really hurt!" she said, rubbing the spot.

"It won't hurt as much as a real sword would," he said, holding his stick at the ready. "Don't dally when you're facing someone. One wrong move and you're done for. That strike would have killed you if it was in a real fight."

They spent the remainder of that day fighting. Corlieu took turns, letting them rest and rub sore and steadily bruising areas while he suffered through their steady stream of threats.

"It hurts, I know," he said at one point as he took a break. "I'm ensuring that it'll sting a bit for the next day or two at least, but no more. It'll remind you of your weak spots and vulnerable areas. You'll remember to watch those spots carefully if the real thing happens."

During his last lesson, he allowed both of them to attack together. Their glee faded quickly when he was able to dispatch them even more easily and occasionally cause them to hit each other.

"Remember this last lesson," he said, plunking his stick down finally and sprawling down on the ground. "When you come face to face with a real fight, you are either going to do one of two things. You might panic and cower and in this case you will be useless and best out of the way. This you must not do, preserve your calm and remember what you have learned today. It isn't much, but it is a start. I will teach you more as time permits but always remember to fight back."

They camped that night in the midst of their practice arena. Corlieu brought out some oil that he had in his bag and gave it to the girls to rub on their bruises. The rest of that night was spent talking about fighting and weaponry. It was easy for Corlieu to answer all their questions and talk about the battles, brawls and fights he had been through. It was amusing because as he talked, he could see looks of admiration in their faces. At one point, Corbella looked puzzlingly at Corlieu.

"One moment," she said standing up and walking around Corlieu. "You're pretty young, aren't you? Certainly not old enough to have possibly been through all these quests and fights you've mentioned. I don't know if there have even been that many chances in the known world to start off with!"

"That's right, and the equipment you mentioned from all these places—how is it possible that you've traveled so much?" asked Meliore suspiciously.

Corlieu sat back and looked from one to the other. He pondered how they would accept the knowledge that he and members of his order had been around for centuries, some like his master for nearly a millennia, and carried over the knowledge they had gleaned from lifetimes of struggle and experience.

"I am not lying to you two," he finally said. "I have been through more than you can imagine and it's been a busy life. I just have been fortunate if you can call it that," he said with a short laugh. "You'll find out if you stick around with me that nothing that I'm telling you is false. Anyways, I do think it's time to get to sleep. Since we don't have a chance at surpassing this army on our way to our destination anymore, we need to hope that we can rely on stealth since they surely will be encamped around the castle."

Corlieu fished stones out of the dying fire and instructed the girls on preparing a bed using them for warmth. Once they were situated, he went walked over to the fire and began preparing his bed. As he pulled out some stones, he thought he could hear them snicker.

"Men don't laugh like that," he said, slightly annoyed.

Echoes of light and luminescence danced around his eyes, changing forms and taking shapes nearly distinguishable before fading off into obscurity. It wasn't frightening or thrilling. It simply was and Corlieu was there watching it. The intensity increased, his vision became less crowded and he witnessed events from his past. His training in the order, his master who recounted the battle of Plataea and the warnings he gave him about the world. That the visible world was always under the direction of other forces, some benevolent and others not so. It was the way of life and it was their duty to ensure that the generations they were born into had the best chance to survive the calamities that came. It was all too much for Corlieu to comprehend, too bizarre and unbelievable until he was initiated in his mid–twenties.

Scenes shifted and he watched himself, a new initiate with his master marching with the Romans in the war against Carthage. It was then that he was able to see the world and what other humans were unable to recognize. The fate of the future hung on the result of this battle and the best result dictated that the Romans had to win. His master confirmed this on the field and together, they managed to secure a very narrow victory and ensure the beginning of Rome's conquest. Corlieu smiled, remembering the victory celebrations in Rome and the accolades of this "Warrior of Africa".

It was a glorious time and a great battle he was witness to so long ago. The vision faded to blackness first and then to slowly rising embers. They flickered majestically, one after the other. They were so close that he could have touched them, but locked in the dream world, he could only stare. More and more came swirling about him. Hundreds, then thousands and tens of thousands swarmed until he was awash in a sea of fire. His skin was on fire and his mind raced, but there was nothing to be done. Stuck, helpless and unable to control the dream, Corlieu endured the fire in torment.

"CORLIEU!"

The voice broke through his mind and the fire shattered. He woke up with a start finding Meliore face to face with him looking worried.

"Thank the heavens you're up," she said with a sigh of relief. "You've been asleep for the past day and were all feverish. We couldn't awaken you and didn't know what was happening."

Corlieu put a hand on his forehead and feeling beads of sweat drip down his back and into his soaked shirt.

"I'll be fine," he said after closing his eyes a moment and regaining his composure. The memory of the fire and its pain were quickly departing and his mind was clearing. At last, he looked around and saw that they were sheltered against a burn out building. He tried to sit up but found his arms and legs were tied together. Puzzled, he threw Meliore a sidelong glance.

"Sorry," she hastily said going over and untying the ropes. "you were thrashing around and we didn't know what else could be done to stop you."

Corlieu said nothing but stood up, shakily at first then with a bit more confidence after testing his limbs. He found a dry shirt from his bag and cast aside his sweaty one before noticing and walking over to Corbella. She was leaning against a ruined doorway, watching the castle intently. She glanced over at him as he came and looked out upon the scene.

Smoke still billowed out of low squat buildings that were scattered around a town center. Stones littered the sidewalk where carts, merchant stalls and random gear from an ordinary day's work lay scattered about. In the distance, probably no more than a half–hour's walk away, loomed a castle. It was built right atop an outcropping from the nearby mountain range and held a dominating view of the countryside with the steep mountains as its backdrop.

"It's been very quiet," she whispered. "When we couldn't awaken you, we continued along the path you indicated and came to this village. We must have been much closer than you thought because we didn't have to continue much further while you slept."

"Where are the horses?" he asked, looked around and finding no trace of them.

"There is a shattered barn next door," Meliore said, nodding to one side. "A few stalls were suitable so we put them up in there."

" Another thing worth mentioning were the horsemen," said Corbella. "This past morning they came riding through here from the castle and I haven't seen them return."

"Corlieu," asked Meliore. "We saw fires coming from the castle earlier today before the horsemen rode by. Could they have been all that was left? I mean, did they abandon the castle?"

"What did they look like? he asked. "Did they have any equipment with them or look forsaken or like they just clawed their way out of a great fight?"

"No, not at all," she said. "They only had lances and were riding at a good pace."

"It's my expectation then that those riders you saw were merely on errands to the supporting castles. Not at all unusual, perhaps requesting more assistance or sending commands from one to another. If that's the case, then they will be returning and we need to find a way to persuade them to take us along."

Corlieu walked to one corner of the room, thinking quietly of various disguises and the chances they had of getting them in. Occasionally he looked up and surveyed the girls who glanced at him in confusion.

"I suppose there's no helping it," he finally said. "You two will have to be a fine pair of nuns trained in healing who have been sent on the rumor of war to assist the injured. Does that work?"

They both nodded.

"Good, I am merely your guard and for the love of the emperor do not mention anything about us tracking them here, nor where you are really from or anything that would give your true identities away. Just address me as Gelleron from the Kingdom of Neapel. Can you two remember that and not blunder?"

"How about we don't address you as anything at all?" asked Corbella.

"Indeed," said Meliore. "We could just call you the Guard."

He looked at both of them in annoyance before throwing up his hands and crouching down into his bags once again and rummaging around for food.

"I imagine that's suitable enough. Luckily Neapel is far away and they might attribute your strange behavior to merely local habit… I hope."

"CORLIEU!" came a shout from behind him. He swung around and saw

Corbella pointing, not to the castle but down the road. *"THE RIDERS ARE COMING BACK!"*

He ran over and peered out the doorway. The land gently sloped downwards to the south and west, providing a great view of the surrounding countryside dotted with patches of forest and large interspersed clearings. The woods were dense, making a dark wall that enclosed farmlands encircling the ruined town they were hiding in. It was difficult to see far since the bulk of the remaining terrain was shrouded in fog that twisted around, revealing patches and covering them back up as quickly. Just out of reach of the fog was a road that split the land in half up to the horizon. Along it, throwing up a small cloud of dust was a mass of quickly moving shapes. Corlieu watched them for a while until they drew closer.

"Are those the riders you saw earlier?" he asked Corbella.

"I think so," she finally said after a brief hesitation. "I mean, I can't be completely certain but that looks like them. Wait…where are you going?"

Corlieu stepped out from the ruins and walked over to the road. He need to get them into the castle before the army renewed their assault upon it. This group of riders, if they were from the castle, would not be able to set out again if it was already under attack.

Course they might just spear me right here. I'll have to see what their initial reactions are when they spot me.

He tucked away his sword as best as he could. It was not easy to hide, even on the best of days, but he wanted to make sure they wouldn't be distracted by it. He loitered in the shade of an overhang while the ground began to quake and the rhythm of hooves increased. Presently, they came up the road. Upon spotting Corlieu, they slowed to a walk and the lead rider approached.

"Who are you and why are you wandering here in my lord's realm?"

Corlieu bowed slightly, keeping one eye on the approaching rider and the guards. Nobody drew a weapon and he was careful to keep his palms up and exposed in a passive sign. Still though, he was ready at a moment's notice and could feel his sword pushing against him when he bowed, almost eager for battle.

"I am Gelleron from the Kingdom of Neapel," said Corlieu. "I was sent on a quest to guard nuns of my order on the way to the service of your lord."

The man's eyes narrowed and he jumped off his horse, walking briskly towards Corlieu.

"What would you know about the needs of my lord?" he asked in an accusatory tone. "Why should we trust you, a stranger out of the wild?"

"Our lands have seen the passing of this army that you are confronting. It's our duty to assist those that fight against it. We have seen what they did to Marseilles on our journeys and are ready to assist however we can."

The man walked up to Corlieu and looked him in the face. His eyes looked from one pupil to the other, possibly searching for lies, nervousness, or ill intent. Corlieu slowed his breathing and quieted his beating heart, allowing himself to be surveyed for endless seconds. Finally, the man nodded.

"You aren't the first one to offer assistance and we are happy to have it if it is my lord's wishes. Where are your companions? We must be quick if we hope to make it back into the castle. Already this fog is blowing back upon us"

"Half a second," said Corlieu, jogging back towards the gutted building.

Chapter 9

The countryside stretched on and up, blackened and littered with wreckage from the passing of the army they had been following. Everything that had stood in their way to the castle had been completely flattened right up to the very trees and stones. It was a devastating sight that reminded Meliore of Marseilles. She had to ride double with one of the riders this time on Stocatta while Corbella did likewise with another. With the threat of attack upon them, Meliore was glad for the protection.

"Tell me about the land you come from?" the rider she was holding onto asked.

"Pardon?" asked Meliore, breaking away from her surveying.

"What is your land like and are the people hospitable?" he prompted.

"Oh, I see. Well…," she stalled a moment and tried to think of something to say.

"Um, yes. It's pleasant enough. The ocean keeps the air cool, even throughout some of the hottest summer months. It's definitely brighter though, the light looks a little bluer than I'm used to up here."

The rider nodded and motioned for her to continue.

"The people too, actually I don't know too much about them. We're limited to the monastery for study and tending to the sick. The people who come in aren't generally in the best moods to talk to."

"I imagine not," said the rider after laughing. "Pardon my constant harassment; I was just curious what things were like beyond the borders of my lord's realm. I haven't traveled far at all and what with all the wanton destruction and waste here from the invaders, I miss the green fields and unsoiled sky."

Meliore sat quietly for a moment, continuing her survey of the land. As they got closer to the castle, the pungent vapors became denser. Gray–black smoke clogged their lungs and watered their eyes. The sights of wreckage and discarded equipment littered the ground.

"Who are these invaders?" she asked presently. "Have you seen of them?"

The rider sat quietly for a moment with his lips pursed.

"I know not. They're odd and have many strange effects. At first when they came and razed the town you were hiding in, we just guessed it was another foreign army on the warpath. Many of the people fled to the safety of the walls and we garrisoned ourselves. Usually, invaders that come by bypass us in favor of easier targets and simple raids on the surrounding towns. However, they laid siege to us and tested our defenses."

It was at this point that Meliore noticed him massaging an area on his right shoulder. He held that arm awkwardly, as if it pained him and continued on.

"I was in the first assault to drive them away," he said. "They are human enough but terribly diseased. Many of their limbs are blackened and covered in boils of some kind. Furthermore, this sickness seems to be easily passed to us. Whenever it seemed that we struck one down, our comrades would find their digits afflicted with it."

"Why did you riders leave the castle? Where did you go?"

"After a few days of this stillness, our lord sent us out to scout what our enemy might be doing and to request additional help from the surrounding towns and castles. It's strange though. Nothing to the north, east and west of us are touched and knew nothing about the army. Only the towns to the south, along the invader's trail of destruction, were ruined. It seemed as though they were coming straight for us."

"TO THE LEFT!" came a shout down the line of riders.

Immediately the whole line drew their weapons and an array of the archers readied themselves. To Meliore's astonishment, her rider was instantly armed and ready, but looking to the right.

"What are you doing, he said left?"

"It could be a feint," he said, scanning the right side of the column. "Never leave your flanks open, even when you think…" he started, but he didn't get a chance to finish.

"INCOMING RIGHT!"

Meliore saw a group of shapes come running through the vapors. They were wordless and soundless with weapons drawn and billowing garments. Before she was aware of what happened, they were beset and the clatter of arms sounded all around her.

"Hold on tight!" said the rider, fending off one of the attackers and goading his horse forward.

Around them she could see shapes fighting and riders falling as they were overwhelmed. A horn blew and the riders pressed forward and tried to escape. The looming walls indicated that they were close to the castle and another horn blew from within and a rain of arrows shot out the nearby attackers. The sounds of creaking and groaning filled the air and the riders rushed through the walls as a company of soldiers rushed out to secure the gate.

"QUICKLY," one of them yelled. *"BEFORE THEY TAKE THE GATE!"*

Corbella was close by, hanging on to the rider in front of her. He helped her to the ground and prepared turn around.

"THIS ISN'T A SAFE PLACE FOR YOU TWO!" he said, yelling and pointing off towards a building. *"GO OVER THERE!"*

Meliore's rider helped her off as well and with polite nods, the riders turned towards the gate ready to fight. They stopped short, however, looking astonished.

"Who is that?" one of them asked.

"It's that man who came with the nuns," the other said. "What is that ridiculously giant sword he's using, though?"

"He's doing a fantastic job with it," said one of the riders, laughing with admiration. "C'mon, we have to help him."

As they departed for the gate, Meliore caught a glimpse of Corlieu. He was standing at the gate, yelling obscenities at a group of soldiers nearby and in pitched battle just under the gate. That was all she saw as more warriors came and shunted them aside in the direction of the building.

*****

Corlieu was deep in thought about his first encounter with the invaders as he followed a set of guards and a captain deep within the confines of the castle. Besides him, also under watch, were the girls. They crossed a large atrium and passed through two grand double doors. A long table was set out and a small group sat at the far end of it. The man at the head wore elaborate robes and was in deep concentration with the man to his right.

"Here are the people you wished to see, my lord," said the captain. "This is the warrior from the south and these two are the healers that he was safeguarding."

The lord of the castle motioned them over to seats and Corlieu waved the girls to fill in the seats at his side. The captain took a seat opposite them and the guards spread out through the room, though two remained on the sides of the lord.

"Welcome," he said. "You come at a very strange and unexpected time. Even though we did send word for help, our envoys didn't get anywhere near the lands you three are from. How did you come to be here?"

"Their order contracted me to ensure their safety," said Corlieu, motioning towards the girls. "The head of the monastery caught news of this invading army as they crossed the sea from the east and we were tasked with following and helping those who fall victim of their might."

"Are you saying that we are weak and in need of help from the whole of the west to thwart these invaders?"

"Of course not my lord," said Corlieu, squirming uncomfortably.

Touchy, isn't he.

"As you well know by now, there is something amiss with these invaders," Corlieu pressed on. "They not only seem to fight but also spread their disease."

"He is right my lord," said the captain. "There is a definite odor of rot by the gates and many of the men who fought there have taken ill."

"Everyone you mean," said the lord. "Everyone except him and the soldiers he was yelling at. Tell me, what right do you have to order my soldiers around?"

"I had to, they are good men but the fighting at the gate was getting desperate and they needed guidance or else there would be fighting, even in here. I have been through very many wars and commanded legions of men in battle before. You'll pardon a commander for finding himself unable to hold his tongue."

"That seems to be the case," said one of the men at the table and Corlieu recognized him as the captain of the riders and one of the warriors at the gate. He coughed violently, but held his composure and kept speaking. "His swordplay was excellent and his command was redoubtable. Though I am certain we could have held the gate without him, it would have been a much tougher fight."

"And what of his sword?" asked the lord. One of the guards rushed forward and presented it. It gleamed in the light and Corlieu smirked as he saw the lord take it and bow under its weight.

"This is a marvelous piece of work, but it is too big and heavy isn't it?" he said, looking astonished at Corlieu. "Such a thing as this could easily be outmatched by something smaller."

"You have to know what you're doing. I have fought in many battles and have much experience even against the finest and most exotic of things with this weapon."

"Show me," said the lord, motioning to one of the captains. "I have never seen something like this in action."

A guard took the sword back to Corlieu who held it aloft and went to meet the captain in the open space near the doors. The captain saluted him and charged with his short sword held aloft and his shield forward and at the ready. The room echoed as he attacked and lunged, swung and struck again and again at Corlieu, who lazily blocked and parried his attacks. Presently, the captain began to sweat and scowl in frustration and his attacks became fiercer and wilder before Corlieu swung in close, using the butt of his sword to crash down on his helmet, blocking his eyes and sending him staggering back.

"Ready?" Corlieu said, holding his sword aggressively. He could feel the giant blade vibrating with the energy in his body and smiled in anticipation. It was always such a great joy to show off sometimes and the battle at the gate was just what he had been waiting for since being woken up. The captain fixed his helmet and set himself at the ready.

Corlieu bore down on him, swinging lightly and dancing his blade from side to side. Twice, he smacked the captain on his arms with the flat side of the blade and pressed down upon him. Again and again, the captain was pushed back, seemingly unable to find a moment to attack or escape the reach of the sword.

"That's enough!" said the lord. Corlieu stopped and withdrew, leaving the sweaty and irritable captain to catch his breath. "Most fascinating," the lord continued. "I have never seen such a thing before with a weapon of that size."

He took his seat back next to the girls and for the first time noticed their dumbfounded looks. It took all his willpower to keep from laughing and looked back at the head of the table. The others, sitting around, cast sideways glances as the lord spoke.

"We have to make use of him. Clearly he has some knowledge pertaining to our situation and a warrior of his standing cannot be discarded. High Constable," he called out and the man at his right stood up. "He is to accompany you and assist in the fight however he may. I don't want any problems with his integration. You must realize he isn't an enemy of the type we're dealing with since he is neither bringing a foulness to the air nor possessing any of the other attributes of these invaders. Understood?"

The lord wrote something down on a paper, grabbed a nearby candle and left an imprint of his ring in the wax he dripped on the paper. The High Constable nodded, taking the paper and walked over to Corlieu.

"This is a warrant allowing you the privileges and rights according to your status and ability. You are to accompany me and are allowed command, but any substantial actions must be approved of first. Understood?"

"Yes," said Corlieu, pocketing the paper. "What of the nuns?"

"They were sent here as healers, right?" said the lord, calling over a group of guards. "Show them to the other healers."

"Can I go with them?" asked Corlieu. "We've been together a very long time and if anything should happen during the battle, I want to be sure they know where to go and what to do to get back to the monastery."

"Yes, of course," said the lord, waving them on. "Proceed as you will."

Chapter 10

The High Constable and Corlieu lead the way back through the atrium and down a few flights of stairs into the castle grounds. Corbella found herself mesmerized by the scene around her. The grounds were flush with peasants, most certainly from the countryside and they crowded into any open corner or spot. Many were weeping, some sagged as they sat, letting their loose limbs cast withered looking shadows on the ground. Everywhere, soldiers filed past on errands. Many of them were younger than she would have expected and their faces were masked with twinges of fear. Overall, they were trapped in a morose, serious world.

"Why are there so many soldiers down here?" she overheard Corlieu asking the High Constable. They argued back and forth for a moment before she saw the High Constable nod and they approached a group of guards, gave orders and walked back.

Corbella watched Corlieu with increasingly surprised appraisal. It was amazing how quickly he made a name for himself in this place. His knowledge seemed to have no limit and she overheard him talking about such things as siege and proper ordering of refugees, rationing and defensive strategy. The High Constable looked severely irritated, probably at the fact that he was ordered to entertain this stranger, but Corlieu's advice seemed to make more sense than annoyance because on a number of occasions, when Corlieu had mentioned something and argued a moment, a set of commands were given and changes were made. Presently, they reached right around to the other side of the castle and entered a large, airy room. Corbella was looking at the room when Meliore reached out and squeezed her arm.

"Corbella, we're at the foot of the castle keep. That fellow in Marseilles told me that the treasure would most likely be here in the lowest floors."

"What do you mean 'most likely,'" Corbella whispered back. "You make it sound like you don't know where…" she started saying, but Corlieu pushed in between them.

"Here," whispered Corlieu, pushing a note into Corbella's hand and closing it and looking at her meaningfully.

"I can't read though…" said Corbella. Meliore shook her head too, staring blankly at Corlieu.

"I'll lure the guards away," said Corlieu, gesturing wildly and pointing south. "Get the treasure, as much as you can, and hang a white sheet with a black line down the middle on the roof of the livery," he continued, now brandishing his fists and making a punching motion. "I'll meet you there as soon as I can. Hide until then."

Corlieu turned and went running back to their escorts before turning a moment and yelling at the girls.

"AND LEARN TO READ SOMETIME!"

Behind him, the High Constable surveying them all with a most bemused expression.

"What on earth was that?" he asked, looking from the girls to Corlieu.

"I told them what to do if one of your guards gets too friendly," Corlieu said with a shallow laugh. "Now, we desperately need to see the battlements. What's going on in the field?"

They walked out without a second look and their voices rapidly faded away. Once again, Corbella found herself in a strange place with only a faint idea of where they were supposed to go or what to do. She wheeled around, grabbing Meliore's arm and pulling her to one side.

"We're here," she said excitedly. "I can hardly believe we made it inside. Now all that's left is to find this glorious end to our poor miseries."

Meliore stammered a second and hung her head.

"That thief in Marseilles didn't tell me what it was. I don't think he even knew himself to be honest. The way he described it, it was just something big and valuable. If it's either of those, then how are we going to escape with something the likes of that?"

"You couldn't tell us that then?" Corbella said indignantly. "We could have planned ahead you know."

"Is it not obvious?" said Meliore with a sigh. "This is a great chance and I don't want it all to end in ruin. Corlieu has been a lot of help and I didn't want to take a chance that he'd abandon us and get it all himself."

While they were talking, Corbella didn't notice a nun walk up and stand patiently, waiting for them to finish. She would have continued on, oblivious to the eavesdropper, if she didn't see Meliore straighten up and warn her with a twitch of her eyes.

"Um…" murmured Corbella turning slowly and glancing at the nun over her shoulder. "Can we help you?"

"Yes actually I do believe I can help you," she said in a soft little voice. "I was assigned to help gather whatever materials you needed. My lady tells me that you two come from along the coast in the kingdom of Neapel. We have never had the privilege of having sisters from such a far place here and we were hoping you would be able to give us some new ideas. What order do you come from if I might ask?"

Corbella felt the muscle at the side of her mouth tighten and she turned to feign a cough and cast a stricken look at Meliore. What on earth were they going to say? She didn't remember any Orders and was too flummoxed to effectively think.

"We're from the Order of the Beleaguered Sheep," said Meliore in a laconic tone, not even glancing away from the interested nun. It was silent for a moment and Corbella blinked, looked at Meliore and mouthed the words she had just said.

"I have never heard of that order," said the nun. "It must be a quite a small community."

"It is, we only come around to local villages when there are large numbers of sick and dying."

"Then why are you all the way over here?"

"That's easy," said Corbella. She turned around and faced the nun. "Some of our order travel from time to time and only appear when we're needed."

"Oh, I see. Then how…" she started, but Corbella cut her off.

"We don't really talk much about our order. We took a vow of…"

"…silence," said Meliore with a sigh.

"I understand," said the nun with a nod. "Please, pardon my intrusiveness."

"Of course," said Corbella. "Now, since you came to help us, there is a task at hand. Do you have any cabbage? That's one of the main ingredients since our order uses as a poultice."

"I've heard of that being used before, but we never used that here and there isn't any in the stores. Usually we just use leeches on swollen areas and stuff fresh wounds to stop the bleeding."

"No, that won't do at all," said Corbella. "We need cabbage."

Again the nun nodded.

"Anything else?" she said.

"Stump water," said Meliore.

The nun looked at her in confusion and Corbella nearly bit a hole in her lip trying not to laugh.

"Like our Mother Superior always said, stump water is the answer. From stiff joints and muscles to purple blotches and oozing sores, the cure is stump water."

"I see, that's going to take a little bit of time to find," said the nun, nodding her head and moving towards the hallway leading outside. As she left, Corbella could hear her musing out loud. "Stump water... I've never heard of such a thing. This must be an incredible remedy... stump water..."

Finally Corbella was able to laugh and Meliore joined in.

"Great job there," Corbella said. "I don't know how long it's going to take for them to find out we're lying out of our backsides, but that was incredible. Where did you get 'Order of the Beleaguered Sheep' from?"

"I simply made it up. We are rather beleaguered sheep ourselves, aren't we? A Anyways, let's go, we don't have much time before we're supposed to signal Corlieu so follow me."

The din of noise faded as they went deeper into the castle and down a flight of stone stairs. They were now underground and all semblance of daylight vanished. A few candles burnt here and there, showing pale outlines of the room and the adjoining hallways. Despite the still air and stagnant nature of the floor, there was a pervasive smell of roses and lavender. As Corbella looked around, she noticed that the floor was littered in a light layer of flower petals.

"Fancy, isn't it?" she said, kicking some of the petals aside. "Where to now?" This place is a little creepy with all of the guards gone and everybody up preparing for the fight.

Meliore didn't say anything for a while. She looked from one way to the other, muttering and ignoring Corbella.

"I remember that there would be a set of spiral stairs somewhere inside the keep, but I can't remember exactly where. He said there would be a hall to the right here, but there isn't one. I guess we should just take one of these doors that could lead us in that basic direction."

They walked generally following a rightward direction. Presently, they came upon an archway with spiral steps leading downwards.

"This is it, let's be off!" said Corbella, starting off down the steps. Meliore put out an arm and halted her though.

"Be careful. I don't know what we'll find down there so watch your feet."

Corbella jogged back up the hallway and grabbed two of the candles.

"Problem solved," she said handing one to Meliore.

Together, they proceeded down the steps and through the doorway in front of them and turned right down a hallway. A few small rooms opened to their left and were stuffed with barrels, utensils and equipment. An acrid smell came out of it and the floor was stained black.

They hurried past these rooms, stopping and checking the floor whenever they got to a new one. They found nothing other than storage and sleeping quarters and as they pressed on their franticness grew. They didn't know how long they had before the other nuns returned raised an alarm. In the meantime Corbella felt as though she was running around a maze and after one last right turn, she came to a frustrated stop

"Meliore! We're right back where we started from. Look, there's the landing there where we came down. Where are we going now, I did not see anything looking like a second set of stairs?"

"I don't understand," said Meliore walking around the room apprehensively. "He said it would be here and not hard to find. We just have to make sure we…"

Corbella was staring out towards the landing, puzzling over the rooms they had been through and where a treasure might be hidden. She didn't take notice of Meliore's silence and was feeling irritable.

"So what now? After all this, was he lying?"

Silence.

"HELLOOOO…" Corbella called out, hearing her voice echo and feeling the eerie emptiness of this level for the first time.

"WAIT, STOP!" came a strangled clamor. *"NO! DO SOMETHING, I'M SLIPPING!"*

Panicked and unsure what was happening, Corbella spun around and held out her candle. She could hear Meliore struggling and cursing somewhere in the darkness, but the light was too dim to make out the room's features.

"HURRY! I'M GONNA FALL!"

Hastily, Corbella covered the length of the room. She stooped down low, hoping that the dim light would warn her of any danger quickly enough for her to react.

"I SEE THE LIGHT. HURRY UP AND GET ME OUT OF HERE!"

Corbella turned about and noticed a deeper darkness in the floor. She made a dash over to it and saw a pair of hands digging into the stone edifice. It was a slight struggle, but luckily Meliore still had the strength to help climb. She collapsed once she was safely back up.

"Why'd you go all the way over here? Especially when you knew the stairway would be like this."

"I was still looking and also thinking about what that fellow said. And no! I didn't think he was lying to us. I just, I dunno. Forgot the details?" she said with a meek shrug.

Corbella didn't say anything. It was best to just let it go. She inched over to the edge and peered down. The opening stretched left and right to the walls, ending in a half circle whose depths the faint candlelight couldn't pierce. At the far left where the edge met the wall, there was a set of stairs that lead straight down.

"Kind of a strange place for a pit, isn't it?" Meliore asked, trying to peer over the edge while maintaining her distance. "No ledge or anything for warning."

Quickly, Corbella swung around and grabbed Meliore. She squeaked in shock and recoiled away from the pit.

"I scarcely know how long it's been since we disappeared from upstairs. I don't know how much time that stump water creation of yours bought us, *BUT THE TREASURE IS DOWN THERE!*" she said excitedly, shaking her.

"Cut it out!" Meliore replied, brushing Corbella off of her and straightening out her clothes. "And it's not just stump water; it's a way of life."

She walked off with Corbella trailing behind and started heading down the stairs. They were moderately well maintained and not terribly slippery, but the length and steepness of it was astonishing and if it wasn't for the wall, Corbella was certain that she would have gotten disoriented and slipped.

They went downwards and onto a landing, then to the right and towards another set of stairs. At what Corbella could guess was the bottom, there was a flickering glow and faint muttering. As she went down, the muttering got louder and occasionally burst into shouts of gibberish and nonsensical raving.

"Wait!" Corbella whispered to Meliore. "Someone's down there! I thought Corlieu was supposed to lure all the guards off?"

"This is some great treasure we're after. There have to be some guards specifically assigned to it who can't be removed or reassigned to anything else."

"Fair enough, what do we do now?" Corbella said creeping a few stairs down and looking around. "It doesn't look like there's any way to get around him. There is just a small hallway and someone sitting and rocking on a chair in the middle of it."

"Someone doing what?" asked Meliore loudly.

Her voice carried surprisingly well and echoed up the stairway. Corbella cringed as she heard the rambling guard stutter and stop talking.

"ELLO?" he called loudly. *"CAN'T COME DOWN HERE TONIGHT, EVERYTHING'S ON LOCKDOWN. COME LATER WITH MORE SALTED PORK IF YOU PLEASE."* Having said that, he went back to muttering and the sound of creaking wood commenced.

Meliore caught Corbella's eye. She incredulously mouthed the words "salted pork? My lord does that sound amazing."

"SHUT YOUR MOUTH YOU!" Corbella whispered furiously, waving her hands in front of her mouth and holding up her fist.

"It's okay," said Meliore and neglecting to whisper. "Can't you hear him? He's had too much beer or ale."

Corbella took a quick peek down the hallway before stepping out and creeping forward a few steps.

"He is just there, rocking back and forth in the middle of the hallway," she whispered. *"I think he's facing away from us but it's too dark and his voice is echoing everywhere."*

"How many doors are there?" asked Meliore.

Corbella was irritated that she wasn't whispering, but took another quick look down the hallway.

"There is only one, but it's all the way at the end," she said, coming back and slumping against the wall. *"We'd have to confront him somehow."*

Meliore stood up and glanced around the corner a moment or two. Before Corbella could said anything, she walked out into plain view and stood in the middle of the hallway. Corbella sat open mouthed, expecting the hear the guard yelling.

"C'mon," she said walking back to Corbella. "I'm quite certain now that he's facing the other way."

They crept over with Meliore in the lead. The man was completely oblivious to them, still mumbling to himself and occasionally taking a large gulp from his flagon. It was not long before they got to the back of his chair and crouched.

"Now what?" Corbella mouthed.

Meliore shrugged and peered over him, then mimed pulling him over with a quizzical face.

Corbella shook her head and stood up, looking over the top of him. He was dirty and ill kept. The smell of rotting sausages, smoke and beer emanated from his every pore. A long spear lay to one side and a small mountain of empty containers gathered around him on the floor. After looking around him, she crouched back down and thought.

Why would they leave this terrible guard here to protect this great treasure? There's nothing keeping anyone from coming through here and stealing some of it.

With that, Corbella gave a gasp and quickly slapped her hand back over her mouth. Meliore looked at her in surprise and held her hands up in question. It was too much to communicate there but it was of the utmost importance.

"How are we going to take the treasure out?" Corbella mouthed and mimed.

Meliore looked back at her, seemingly uncomprehendingly and mouthed something back to her. Corbella put her head in her hands in frustration. They were getting nowhere fast and needed to knock this poor guard over so they could talk and move freely. She reached down and picked up the spear, ready to crack it over his head, but Meliore got in the way just as she was about to close her eyes and swing it.

"NO!" she mouthed, holding her hands out, completely blocking the way.

Corbella was on the verge of knocking out both of them in irritation when Meliore held up a finger, grabbed the back of the guard's chair and spun him facing the other way when he leaned back and took a drink. Corbella scrambled to get behind him, letting the spear fall and collecting herself a second. The noise from the falling spear made the guard rock his head back and once again he yelled for salted pork, this time down the wrong end of the hallway and went back to mumbling to himself.

Meliore motioned to him, shrugged with a grin and started walking to the end of the hallway. Corbella caught up and punched her in the shoulder.

"Good job," she said. "I was ready to put a dent in his head."

"So I saw, but I figured since he looked loopy enough anyways that he wouldn't notice being spun around."

They reached the end of the hallway and put their hands on the door.

"Is this it?" Corbella asked. "It's the only door here."

"Yes, this is exactly where I was told. Just on the other side is what we're seeking.

"This is almost too easy," said Corbella. "One drunken guard? Unlocked doors and torches to light the way down here? Something's not right."

Meliore opened her mouth but just gulped and nodded.

Chapter 11

With a nod and thrust, Meliore helped Corbella push open the doors. They swung inwards with a painful groaning noise like an old man bending over. Wide–mouthed, she waited in anticipation of some glorious treasure to graze her eyes.

Nothing…

"What…?" she said, looking over at Corbella.

Her enthusiasm faded rapidly and her outstretched arms quivered in shock. The room was nearly empty and there certainly wasn't anything of apparent value in there. Nothing glittered gold or silver; nothing reflected the torchlights with red and green hues of rubies and emeralds. It was barren except for a cage in the middle of the room.

Corbella ran to the side and came back with a candle. Together, they walked into the room and closed the doors behind them.

"Maybe that cage is golden?" Meliore said hopefully. "There has to be something, or else, why was that guard there?"

"It could have been a trick, some sort of a diversion," Corbella said vehemently. "I knew this was too easy."

"But…" started Meliore. "Wait, there's something in the cage."

Corbella strode over and held the candle aloft. They both looked in and saw a thin figure.

"Hello?" Corbella called out. "What are you doing here?"

The figure walked over slowly on thin bare feet that made barely a noise on its metal floor. Long dark hair covered his face and he seemed to be coddling himself increasingly tightly with each passing step.

Meliore was stunned into silence and turned to look at Corbella.

"What is this?" she asked. "Is it even a boy….or a girl?"

"I…can't…tell…" she said, shaking her head. "Sort of looks like a boy…"

"Maybe he's worth something?" Meliore said, looking him up and down.

setting us up for slaughter without knowing it. Still, why would they be after a treasure? They have no use for material possessions, not even food. If only I knew who the leader controlling them was….

"What about the supporting castles?" asked Corlieu. "Are they under attack as well?"

"No, that is the strange thing," said the High Constable. "Our riders managed to break the lines earlier and found our two allied castles undisturbed. They sent reinforcements to try and drive away the enemy yesterday, but their combined forces seemed to have been no match for this threat. When we heard the sound of battle we sent out our soldiers but they were soundly defeated. Since then, we have only stood in defense and only one other sortie has managed to break out and back again.

"Sir," said one of the guards, breaking rank and speaking directly to Corlieu. "I was with the force that fought when the other castles sent forces to break the siege. What are these things? They are clothed in this vapor as though it comes straight out of their skin and they are covered in sores and blotches. The sight and rotting smell almost…"

The High Constable went to comment angrily at the soldier's ramblings for interrupting them, but Corlieu held him back. He could see that the guard was frightened and meant no disrespect, but merely as any frightened man would was seeking assurance.

"It is difficult to describe what they are. Not quite human and not quite dead, but they are not here to seek your life, nor anyone's here in particular though they wouldn't mind taking it if they had to."

"It sounds like you know of them?" asked the High Constable. "How does one so young as yourself have such a breadth of information?"

"It has been a ceaseless life," said Corlieu. "I had no privilege and many tough instructors. I have met these things in the northeast, though never in such numbers as this. To tell the truth, the fact that so many of them are here disturbs me greatly."

"There is some greater force at work then?" asked the High Constable. As he did, Corlieu could feel the ears of the nearby soldiers straining to pick up every word he said.

"Yes, what that mission may be, I know not but this is not an ordinary army knew we had to be careful of brigands and thieves, let alone wildlife. Meliore here never traveled, but I was able to. Always by boat though, never left Genoa by land."

"The land has changed a lot since I came this way last, but never the stars and sea. Whatever may come to pass, they are comforting in a changing world."

"What are you Corlieu?" she asked suddenly, turning to look at him. "The world doesn't change much at all in a lifetime. If I was to warrant a guess, I'd say you weren't any more than about 25 years old, but you know more than some of the sages I've known. Even though you have made a number of spectacular claims, I haven't seen anything that would lead me to believe you weren't everything you say."

Corlieu scratched his head and thought. He didn't know if he'd want to explain the full extent of himself and the order without a lot of questions and confusion. As much as he couldn't sleep, he didn't feel like spending the entire night talking about his centuries of duty.

"Don't worry about it, it's been a long life and I've never skipped a chance to learn everything I…"

Corlieu stopped whispering and froze. The steady wind had suddenly stopped and he could feel the air suddenly grow heavy around him.

"What's going on?" whispered a frightened Corbella. "The hairs atop my head are standing on end!"

He slowly raised his head and looked down the mountainside. A sliver of a moon was high in the sky, providing little illumination to the lands below. Even so, the light was sufficient enough for him to be able to see the fields they crossed earlier that evening. Far in the distance, from the direction of the castle but steadily increasing came a wave of mist. League by league, the land was enveloped as it crept in their direction.

"Corlieu…" said Corbella in frightened voice.

"Be silent, don't dare to say another word," said Corlieu urgently.

He felt helpless but there was nothing to be done. Their encampment was a good hiding place, it was out of the way and relatively inaccessible. However, if that was the besieging army coming in their direction then poor terrain wouldn't be able to defend them at all.

Corlieu had no idea how much time had passed. It felt like forever that he lay, watching that wave coming straight towards them. Leagues dropped to fractions and still it came on ceaselessly. The mist, the same type that washed against the castle wall covered the entire horizon before him and it came nearly up to the mountainside, encompassing the entire valley. Then, when they were close enough where he was certain he could see individual shapes inside of it, the fog suddenly ceased and poured off to the east, never coming any closer to them.

"I need to go," said Corlieu hastily, getting to his feet as soon as mist had passed and wrapping up his gear.

"Wha…what?" said Corbella, getting to her feet as well and looking frightened. "Where are you going?"

He went to pack up his blankets and instead gently put them on Meliore and threw one into Corbella's arms. He was thinking fast, oblivious to Corbella for the moment.

That army is on a mission elsewhere, or certainly they would have found us. But where? There is nothing around that would…

And all at once, he knew where they were going.

"I'll be back," he said before hastily running down to his horse and taking off across the moonlit forests.

Chapter 14

Corlieu rode quickly and without much caution. His mind was racing and speed was the only thing that could keep him sedate at the moment. The army was coming for them, that was for sure. That force that was besieging the castle was clearly after that boy and him. There was no mistaking that fact anymore. Maybe they kidnapped him for ransom, perhaps or for something more nefarious. Ideas both probable and highly unlikely popped about, but he shook his head and cleared them out. Whatever the reason was, it held little bearing on what he was now facing.

He had a bad feeling he knew not only what they were facing, but that the only thing that could draw them away was the sanctuary of his master. If the army set off on some other task, then he could rely the keepers of the dwelling for supplies, direction, and advice.

If they did not however....

In the distance he thought he could see the clouds and vapors of the army always just out of reach. He wasn't sure if they were illusions or not, and he never was able to come to a definitive answer. Still though, the sanctuaries relied on incredible secrecy and had always been able to outsmart even the most avid of explorers and conquerors from the past. Why should it fail now?

Then with a wave of dread, Corlieu remembered that his usual sanctuary was discovered and wherever his secondary hideaway was, it also came under attack. Only the remarkable forethought of his Arger provided him with that river escape. He was certain that his master's sanctuary was secure or abandoned at the least. There was only one way to find out though, and with that in mind he pressed his horse forward as fast as he dared.

Corlieu trotted up slowly, crossing an open patch of land and finding a place to leave his horse. The barb at first snorted and tested his knot by chewing and pulling at some of the ropes. It held, however, and the horse simply contented himself with eating the grass nearby his feet. Confident that he would remain now, Corlieu set on his way up the slope leading to his master's sanctuary. Even from far away, he could see something was wrong and a lump began to grow in his neck. The seamless hills were broken open and the foundations it hid were plainly visible. Littering the night skies of the world were multitudes of birds. As Corlieu climbed, he could see they centered around the ruins. He knew what to expect but his mind held out hope that the sight before him was simply a lie. His master had to survive, someone like him could not die.

As he at last stole through the broken sanctuary doors, he knew the worst had come to pass and the defenders had fallen. In the history of the order, there had been instances where sanctuaries were found, sometimes looted or destroyed along with the inhabitants. Corlieu had never seen it in person however and the sight nearly stopped his heart. The tomb where his master laid was split open and ruined.

Corlieu walked up slowly to the remains. Thin beams of starlight shone down through broken parts of the ceiling and detailed the wreckage. A glint of gold caught his eye and he stood there, seeing the ring of his master and certain that it was he that laid there looking as though he was still in his sleep, but Corlieu saw the fatal wound in his side and knew that all life had passed from him.

It was a crushing blow to see him, the famed Warrior of Africa, dead. To know that someone of such knowledge and ability, a fighter and scholar who had lived through nearly two and a half millennia of earth's history and always had the right answer for the situation was now dead, had died unable to defend himself, was simply too much to bear.

He didn't know how long he stood there like a tree, limbs frozen and mind lost in memory. At present, he shook his head and cleared his mind. His master had a saying for things that he now remembered and repeated in his head as he made to leave.

"It's simply the will of all things."

Corlieu nodded his head and covered his master with his cloak. It was only then that something else caught his eye and he swung around on the defensive as a figure stood up.

"Robert Corlieu, it is good to see you," came a voice. As he walked over, hands open in a gesture of peace, his outline was defined. Heavy furs and a long mustache, leather armor underneath and two heavily curved blades gave his identity away.

"Axio Talphon," Corlieu said excitedly, feeling a rush of relief flow over him. It was he, an Axio. One of the mighty sleeping kings of the order, awakened only when their lands were threatened or great need beyond the power of the ordinary order members drove them. Talphon was one such member, but his lands were far to the northeast and his appearance, though not unpleasant, was certainly odd.

"It is good to see you Axio, I feared the attackers were still close at hand."

"I must say that it is good to see you too old friend and it's saddening what came to pass here. I never imagined that someone of such renown could pass on in such a manner."

"What happening?" asked Corlieu after a few moments of silence. "I was awakened early and my sanctuary was attacked as well. There's something that's going through the land as well spreading disease and sickness when they aren't outright killing in a quest for something. I know if you're here, it's a serious matter to have brought you all the way from the frozen lands."

"Corlieu, you know the purpose of our order, correct?" asked Talphon.

"Of course," he responded, struck by the strangeness of the question. "We are to help guide the course of history and ensure that the world has the best chance to survive, even if that means choosing from the least of evil paths."

"A typical answer, spoken word for word right from the Order's literature," Talphon said dismissively. "Do you understand what exactly that means, however?"

Corlieu stuttered a second, trying to find a way to compress the purpose he served into a few words.

"It means control," finished Talphon. "Our purpose is to control the history of this world."

"That makes sense," nodded Corlieu. "It sounds a little grim the way you put it. It lacks the finesse that we have to actually put into the major events but it's essentially correct."

"It's more than correct," said Talphon with a laugh. Corlieu winced, feeling the sanctity of his master's deathbed slightly violated by the echoes of mirth. "It is what we are supposed to do. In all our years however, how successful have we been having to pick from the lesser of evil paths that the world must walk down?"

"We've been successful enough," shot back Corlieu. "A good portion of the knowledge and good from the past has survived through to this generation with our help. It will continue I hope to whatever future there may be."

"I don't know about that," said Talphon walking over to the tomb and laying his hand atop Corlieu's cloak. "As the centuries progress, I'm losing more and more faith in the world."

"What are you proposing?"

"The time for the Order as we know it is passing. It is too chaotic and too vast now to be properly controlling the way things are."

"Are you proposing that we take more control? Limit the population?"

"Yes, we simply have to. It's necessary for the future that we take more control and do some good in this world."

Corlieu stood and wavered a moment. It made logical sense, most of the decisions he's been a part of had no real good, viable selection. Either the destruction of one city, empire or way of life instead of another. If they took control however…

…*No.*

"What was that?" said Talphon, slowly walking over.

"We can't do that," Corlieu said shaking his head. "We are protectors and guides, not rulers. It's a part of our code, we know that any power like that is a threat that only brings suppression."

As he was saying this, Talphon slinked slowly over. Corlieu was unaware, deep in thought, and didn't notice the change growing upon Talphon. His shadow had grown and encompassed his face. The form he wore, as one of the great Axio's of the order was slipping away.

"I can't agree with that," stated Corlieu. He looked over just in time to see the pair of notched blades swing to life and had to spring backwards to avoid it. Whistles cut the air as Talphon, now grown and transformed into a hideous menace leapt full upon Corlieu. He barely had time to draw his sword before the twin blades were crashing down upon him.

"WHAT ARE YOU DOING?" shouted Corlieu in shock.

"I knew you wouldn't agree. Your master wouldn't have I was sure. Always the kind who believed in the good of the world, but you?! You have seen the actions we had to take and the lives that the world has consumed for nothing. There is no hope for the future unless we rule it."

"That is not our way!" shouted Corlieu, dancing his blade off Talphon's and driving him back slightly. "It will only lead to ruin for everyone!"

"Then I will have to kill you too," said Talphon with a sigh. "You are a great order member and could have helped immensely if you only saw the righteousness in the way I see things."

"You killed my master?" said Corlieu, too shocked to react or parry the next attacks. The twin blades missed fatal marks, but still hacked into his armor and pierced deep into his thigh.

"A new power is arising from the old Order," said Talphon. As he said this, the sky darkened and the shades of warriors grew from the shadows around him. They blocked the door with long spears begun pressing upon him. "If you are standing in its way, I will have to eliminate you."

Frantic, seeing only moments before his death, Corlieu sprang into action. He stood little chance fighting one of the Axio's, let alone in a ruined sanctuary with enemies in all directions. When the spears, thickest at the doorway, were almost upon him, he swung his blade in the all cleaving arc he perfected and for the faintest of moments, cleared a path through them.

"You will not succeed!" yelled Corlieu, plunging bodily upon the shades. They fell back and he made for the entrance, dashing through it and running headlong along the slope. Around him, the shadows of the land were sprouting shades and the night skies were clouding over in that fog he had grown so accustomed to seeing.

He heard the thunder of hooves behind him and turned to a highly welcomed sight. His horse, running panicked came at full speed over to him. Corlieu saw with some exasperation that it had crewed through the tie rope and mangled the reigns, but that hardly mattered at this moment.

"EASY…," he yelled to his horse as he pulled alongside, snorting and looking scared. Corlieu wove his hands into the mane and, using the majority of his remaining strength, kicked a leg up and swung onto the back. He laid full upon the neck in desperation a moment before pushing himself backwards and sitting up. The fog was heavy about them and the din of voices and arms was thick in the air. He lead his horse away from the barely visible mountains and across an open plain. He had to lose the army before returning to camp, regardless of his injuries and hope that his strength would hold out long enough.

As the earth flew past underneath him, he could feel wounds on all sides of his body. As much as they protested, he had to keep focused and not lose his balance. There would be no chance of getting back upon the horse, or even getting up if he fell. The army was still behind him, falling back steadily but ready to jump on him if the chance came.

How could you… someone like you, and Axio ought to know better! I can't believe you could do such a thing as this, Talphon.

With that in mind, another thought crossed his head. He stood no chance against him. The only other person who could defeat an Axio in open combat was another. The only other one rested in a mountain on the other side of the Roman peninsula, Axio Fredoric Barbarossa.

Corlieu knew he just had to get there first, and clung tightly to his horse's mane.

Chapter 15

When Corlieu had suddenly ridden off in pursuit of the army, Corbella found herself with nothing to do but sit and watch his shadow disappear into the distance. For a long while she was unable to find a way to situate herself and shifted from one uncomfortable position to another.

Why for the love of Peter did you leave me all alone here....

She felt very afraid. In her current state everything felt like an enemy. The trees twitched from the cold gusts, pulling her concentration from one moving patch in the semi–darkness to another. Her heart beat mercilessly and she found herself remembering when she was very young in her room at night. Meliore's mother always told stories and left a candle burning to comfort them when she slept over. Her mother however did none of these things. She was left alone in the darkness, just as she was now.

There is nothing out there, just have to calm myself.

But there were things out there as she was just learning. Her brother, the pursuing castle knights, whatever the army was and anything else she had yet to learn. When she ran away from her wedding, she never anticipated being in the kind of situation she was in. What she expect exactly, she didn't know. Of course it made sense that Meliore and her couldn't stay in Genoa forever, but what they were going to do then was such a tough question to answer at that time. Furthermore, everything she had gone through only made the answer that much more difficult to find.

Alone against the mountains with an ill cousin and foreign stranger is not how I imagined I would end up.

She thought about how long it was since the night they met Gennaro. If it wasn't for Corlieu, they might still have enough money to be running around and sleeping comfortably as long as their disguises held. A wave of anger hit her and the feeling was shocking. She knew that they might have been burnt to death if they were in their rooms that night, and despite their first encounter with Corlieu made him out to be a thief, he was proving to be a loyal and powerful friend to have around.

Meliore stirred in her sleep, twisting and kicking Corbella. Instinctively, Corbella yelped and raised her hands, seeking to hit her back like they always did when they shared beds. It took all of her effort to restrain herself and she thumped her fist into the ground. Now was not the best time to be hitting each other, especially when she was recovering from that wound.

"I suppose this is what it's like to be in charge," she muttered to herself contemptuously and stared up at the stars before nodding off.

Morning was approaching and the first rays of light greeted a morose looking Corbella. She was cold and disgruntled from checking Meliore's condition all night and had to sacrifice her best blankets to keep her warm. The wound did look much better since Corlieu treated it, but after one curious look she figured it was best to leave it alone and let time do its work.

Still though, when Meliore awoke and stretched, looking warm and refreshed, she seemed to take little noticed of the difficult night Corbella went through.

"What's for breakfast, is there anything to eat?" she asked.

"Good morning to you too," Corbella muttered. "No, not unless you want some biscuits."

"I hate those. They're starting to remind me of the wafers my mother would serve for those boring Sunday family lunches," said Meliore sitting up and yelped sharply. She cursed and laid back down gingerly. "Forgot about that. Well, is there anything?"

"Please," said Corbella exasperatedly. "That's all any of us have to offer and could you relax? It has been a devil of a night and the last thing I want is you to hurt yourself anymore."

"Pardon me," said Meliore in a sultry attitude. "I was just asking, no need to get irritable."

Corbella rummaged through her backpack in silence and came over with some of the biscuits that she still managed to keep in her bag. They were bland and tasteless now that she thought of it, but they were better than nothing after all.

"Here," she said. "Enjoy because it's all we have."

Meliore picked one up and looked at it suspiciously before handing one over to the waking boy. He looked at it, sniffed and ate slowly. Their actions annoyed Corbella, who was already trying desperately to restrain her growing irritation with her cousin. She knew that, as the children of luxury, they had forfeited a great deal of comfort in order to live on their own. Corbella was proud of the way she handled herself so far. Life had been tougher than she anticipated, but she just took it in stride and kept on going. It appeared that the same was not true for Meliore however. Even after breakfast, her mood did not appear to improve and it clashed with Corbella in growing viciousness.

The primary stoker of Meliore's problems seemed to be the pain associated with her wound. Try as Corbella might, she could not explain away the fact that there was nothing she could do to help her. The growing frustration at the situation and the lack of Corlieu to mitigate their tempers finally began to boiled over.

"You know this is all your fault," said Meliore after a long silence between arguments.

"How do you figure that?" snapped back Corbella.

"Right now, I could be at home married to some marvelously strapping lord of Venice, happy and peaceful without a care in the world. But instead, you haul me along with you because you didn't like your husband. Now we're alone out here with these to eat," she said, throwing a half–eaten biscuit down the slope and yelping in pain, "and nothing to look forward to."

Corbella sat stunned and looked slowly towards Meliore.

"Anything else you want to blame me for?"

"Yes, this great treasure is just this stupid boy. We can't understand him, he hasn't done anything for us and we're probably abandoned out here. Corlieu isn't going to stick around with us, a pair of girls, one wounded mind you, with biscuits and a boy who's so thin it looks like he has had nothing but a single biscuit to eat his entire life."

"I can hardly believe you Meliore!" shouted Corbella. "You didn't have to come, you knew it would be hard and you insisted on bringing this boy along! Yet you believed that somehow we'd ride a golden cloud through all of this and live a magical life out here in the wild!? Why, what ideas have you come up with to help?"

Meliore recoiled at the ferocity of Corbella's words. Instead of pacifying her, this only drove Corbella on.

"You were the only one who knew what the treasure actually was!" she shouted, getting to her feet and stumbling a second. "Did you share this with me? Did you tell Corlieu? Did you do anything other than make us believe that it might have been some great glorious thing? Not once."

"I really didn't know either…" said Meliore in a small voice. "Hey, wait. Where are you going?"

Corbella grabbed an overcoat off of Meliore and the stick Corlieu made for her to practice with and walked away.

"I don't know where I'm going," she spat back. "To think and keep myself from poking another hole in you most certainly."

She plugged her ears as she walked down the mountain slope, finding the place where their horse was tied. After a moment she mounted and walked off, hearing the shouts of Meliore die away behind her. She walked a little, coming up to Stocatta and leaning on him like she always did with Mercurie. Her gaze drifted out across the land. Something was moving, ever so slowly. It was like an insect, making its way towards them. She squinted at it and jumped as Stocatta gave off a loud whinny. Corlieu had returned, but her joy had soured as they drew closer. His horse had dipped, letting him slide off softly onto the ground before walking off and eating grass next to Stocatta. He was a mess of cuts and wounds. Dirt matted his face and he weakly tried to get up before crumpling down to his side. Corbella ran over and tried to help him up. She tried desperately, but without result. Finally, she heard him grunt and put his arm over her shoulder.

"Like this…," he said exasperatedly. "Now stand."

Together they hobbled up to the encampment.

"*CORLIEU!*" shrieked Meliore, getting up painfully and walking over to the crumpled figure.

"Water," was all he could say to her as Corbella dragged him up to the spot they had slept.

Meliore came running to them in a moment with a water bladder. He drank quickly, not minding a little that spilt off to the side. He stopped and she took it back.

"I'm glad to see you're alright," he said with a weak smile.

He went silent and closed his eyes. Corbella became very nervous and shook him.

"Corlieu? Corlieu? You're not going to die are you?" Meliore asked. "I don't want to see someone die again in my arms please!"

"No, I'm not finished yet," he said opening one eye and smiling. "Only need to rest awhile."

They sat there in silence, hearing his breathing slow and steady. Corbella didn't know what to do and looked around for answers. The boy was sitting up, watching the two of them in vague comprehension. She wanted to shout at him to do something, but it would have been to no avail. His inability to understand only increased her frustration.

"I need you to do something for me," said Corlieu suddenly. "Heat some water and wash off my wounds, especially this," he said holding up his leg and showing a gigantic gouge. "Next, bring my bag next to me and find a squat jar with thick amber paste in it. It's the same that I used on Meliore. Put it on as many wounds as you can manage, then cover it with a strip of cloth and hold it until it is attached."

Corlieu began to slip off into sleep, his eyes rolling backwards and words slurring.

"Don't waste it all…"

Corbella stared down at him uncertainly until he began to snore ever so softly. She gave a uneasy laugh and Meliore and her went to work. They prepared a fire and sat silently as the water began warming. She was still irritated and did not wish to talk. Within her, she felt swelling sensations of anger and nausea advance and retreat, but always getting stronger. Finally, she couldn't stay seated anymore and stood up.

"Where are you going?" asked .

"You can handle this yourself," said Corbella. "I just need to get away for a little."

She plugged her ears as she walked down the mountain slope, finding the place where Stocatta was tied. After a moment she mounted and walked off, hearing the shouts of Meliore die away behind her. She didn't know what had gotten into her, but she knew she had to get away for a little. Having a wounded Corlieu in her arms reminded her of the dying brigand. Her nerves were rattled and she needed to go out and calm herself.

Corbella trotted on and stopped to look back at the mountain range. She didn't plan on going far, but since Corlieu had returned, she felt as though she could risk going a little further. Not knowing exactly what propelled her on, she studied their hiding spot while she pulled out her hat. After tucking all of her hair into it and donning the male persona she was partially adept at by now, she set off. First at a trot, then at a canter.

Chapter 16

Corbella had a lot of difficulty believing the short amount of time it took for everything to take place. It was morning and scarcely the day before she found herself being escorted into the castle with high hopes and dreams of a wealthy future without interference from her family. Now however she was climbing an innumerable set of stairs carved into the side of a jutting pillar of earth.

During the night she was sure this is where she had thought she had seen lights and in her situation had set off in that direction hoping that the layout and look meant a remote monastery. It would be the only source of help they would get this far in the wild lands. What else could any of them hope to do to survive? They had no provisions or any purpose at the moment, so in desperation she had decided to risk setting off towards the flickering night lights.

She never really knew what to expect when she found the source of the lights. Only her companion's desperate straits had driven her to do anything at all. In the wild country, she knew there was an extraordinary amount of risk appealing to strangers for assistance, but it couldn't be helped. She was also goaded into accepting the risk because the one monastery she had been to had monks who spoke the same language as the boy. Of course, she had no idea for sure.

It sounded basically the same, how different could languages be?

The morning sun had nearly ruined her hopes of finding the place until she found the pinnacle of earth and a set of stairs leading up them. Those stairs were now the ones that she was climbing up, two hundred and fifty nearly vertical steps to the top that she climbed on all fours. She didn't trust herself to stand up all the way as the drop–off was daunting.

At last, the top….

Corbella rested a moment, head down on the ground not really caring if her face got dirty. She had seen the archway above her and knew she had indeed come to a monastery. It was perfect, exactly what she needed the most in the world right now. Safety, assistance and hopefully provisions. She had no idea what they could do for Corlieu, but at the very least some help would lift Meliore's mood.

She heard a voice nearby and looked up. A man was standing in front of her, looking down puzzled. He didn't look like a monk or priest, at least anything like one she had seen. Maybe they dressed differently in this land. In her fatigue, she had no idea why she didn't say anything reasonably intelligible. Perhaps it was the fact that she had ridden the whole way here with a certain annoying phrase the boy had been saying in her head, but she said whatever it was to him.

The reaction was startling and immediate. The man jumped in shock and yelled before pulling out a dagger and thrusting it at her. Corbella was shocked as well and rolled out of the way to dodge the attack.

Oh heavens, what did I say?

He continued yelling and struck again with his dagger. His face was red with rage and he was aiming to kill. Despite her fatigue, she was able to evade long enough to scramble up and face him. The only thing she had was the stick that Corlieu cut for her to train with. In the franticness, she squeeze her eyes shut as the man launched forward again and pulled out the stick. In one fluid movement, she swung it in front of her hoping to merely keep the man back. Instead, felt the stick shudder as she hit something and opened her eyes just in time to see the man hit the ground with a grunt and lay still.

Corbella noticed that her hands were shaking hard and crouched down, trying to steady herself. She didn't know why exactly, but this fight was more shocking than when Meliore and her had to fight the castle guard. Maybe it was the shock of the encounter, or her already tired state that did it, but she found herself fighting back a wave of vomit.

What kind of place did I wander into and was it what I said that did it?

She gulped and looked at the man, face down on the ground. She contemplated going back to camp for a moment. If her first meeting here went this badly, what good could she honestly hope to do for her companions here? It was a useless, foolish thing for her to press on.

As her nausea receded however, she stood up and leaned on her stick with a sigh. Going back to camp really wasn't an option. Corlieu was in serious condition, even if he was going to survive and Meliore was still far from well. In their haste to escape from the besieged castle, they had little time to get any provisions. It would be up to her anyways. It was with this acknowledgement that she grabbed the legs of the man and started to drag him out of sight.

I wonder where I hit him? If only I hadn't closed my eyes, that would have been a great spot to remember....

A yell came from behind her and she spun around, seeing a what looked like a family rushing out of the monastery at her. Corbella let the man's feet fall and ran, just remembering to grab her stick at the last moment. Unless she wanted to run back down the stairs, she had to duck around them. Holding her stick horizontally, she made for the doorway. She heard a whistle as the woman swung a heavy looking bag at her and side stepped just in time and made it through. The children however had found a mud puddle and took to pelting her with great globs. One smacked her in the face and she swore as she ran into the monastery halls.

She looked left and right, seeing only empty rooms and sick people. A few of the doors she tried were locked and at every step she was certain she could hear onrushing feet behind her. Presently, she reached a great polished door that opened with a push. Her feet caught on a high threshold and she flailed, sending her stick flying and landed in the room on her side.

"...can I be of service?" came a confused voice.

Corbella propped herself up, panting for breath and reaching for her stick. The person inside was dressed in the fashion of a friar. He looked as though he had been busy over a collection of books before she barged in. She made to stand up but found her legs too shaky and merely held the stick at him and tried to utter the phrase the boy had been saying.

There was silence in the room as the friar stared at her, wide–eyed. Corbella gulped, wondering if she had the strength to fight off another person. Her wonder turned to confusion however, because the friar broke out into heavy laughter.

"You understand?" she asked.

"Certainly, but the question is do you understand what you just said?" he responded, wiping a tear from his eye.

"No! I have no idea, what does it mean?"

"You just asked in absolutely terrible Greek for some privacy to use the chamber pot, or the equivalent of that. If you are that desperate just to relieve yourself then I would hate to see what you are like when something serious happens."

Corbella was absolutely shocked. The boy was Greek and had needed to relieve himself the entire time. She scratched her head wondering why he needed permission and in the process, a full length of blond hair fell out from under the hat and swung in front of her face.

"If you please my lady, I would recommend that you wait until I can show you to a proper place to relieve yourself."

"Oh no," she said shaking herself out of thought and slowly sitting up. "I haven't the need, not for that at least. I just need your help."

"If you don't know that language, then how did you come to know that phrase?" he asked, intrigued.

"One of my companions speaks only it and there isn't one of us who knows what he is saying. That phrase is something he's been saying for a long time now and we all thought it was something more urgent than that."

"It all depends on how long one has been waiting!" said Bartal. "If the poor fellow has been unable to go, then it is urgent indeed."

"It's scarcely as urgent as the rest of our problems," she said.

"How so?"

Corbella hesitated a moment, wondering how much she could say and if any of their adventure would get her into trouble with the friar.

"Two of my companions are injured, one grievously. We were pursued into the mountains to the north by an army and two groups of cavalry. They haven't found us when I last left, but we are stranded without supplies, help and I haven't any idea what to do. The third companion is useless because we don't understand each other. He's the one who has been saying that phrase I just said."

"How far is your party?" he said, rising up suddenly and looking excited.

"You want to help us?" asked Corbella a little taken aback. "Not that I don't appreciate it, but why?"

"Numerous reasons," said the friar standing up and starting to organize his desk. "First off, you all sound doomed without me. Unless you returned to the castle, you would be hard pressed to find another town or monastery before you all perished. Secondly, I study the language your companion supposedly speaks and have never had the chance to practice with someone. The whole reason why I came to this monastery was to study their collection of Greek books. The fools though, this is a different dialect and completely useless to learn from."

Corbella rose up slowly, leaning on her stick.

"We are encamped a deal of a way against the mountains, it's not walking distance by any means."

"You rode?" he asked.

"Yes," she said. "I fear however that my horse can't support both of us the whole distance."

"I wouldn't ask such a thing," he said clapping his hands together. "If you are all in the dire straits that you made it seems, then you are in need for more than just me. I'll bring enough supplies along for all of us to last a fair while, just one last thing I need to make certain of…."

He looked at her and said something incomprehensible. All Corbella could do was stare back at him in confusion.

"Are you absolutely certain that that sounds like the language the member of your party has been speaking?" he asked.

"It sounds just like it," was all she could say. "I don't know any of it but it sounds really similar."

"Excellent!" he said, sticking out a hand. "Friar Bartal, at your service. I look forward to meeting this member of your group."

"Corbella," she said. "Where are your horses and supplies kept? I didn't see anything as I rode up here?"

"There is a small livery barn a short distance away. It's to the south however and you wouldn't have had need to pass it on your way here. There should be a store of food at the barn we can put on the horses."

As he said this, he was hurriedly collecting books and put them into a great bag that he swung around his back. He froze a moment, looking at her and let his bag gently fall.

"I believe you are in need for a different disguise. Here," he said, rummaging through his bag and pulling out a large cloak. "You will have to dispense with the hat so you can use your hood.”

He took a few moments, straightening the black cloak and fastening her hair back. Corbella cringed and squirmed, feeling as though he was trying to pull her hair out.

“And now for the final touch,” he said pulling a small bag out from one of the closets and tying it to her back underneath the cloak.

“There we are, now you have the hump of a great scholar. A brazen little crone you have become!”

“I am not a crone,” Corbella said in mixed anger, reaching behind her and tugging at the bag.

“Of course you are not,” he said slapping her hand down. “But one you must be nonetheless if we are to escape without any more of your fool hearty running about. Now let’s move, the morning is waning away and it sounds like your companions are in need.”

Chapter 17

Corlieu was aware that he was dreaming this time. He had no idea how, he always dreamt completely believing whatever was going on and forgetting the waking world. This was different and he strode through semi–transparent darkness with complete awareness in his mind. That's not to say that he knew what was going on or where he was going. His body was invisible and he was unable to determine how he was able to move or look around. A few times already he stopped and changed direction, first this way and that. No matter where he went however, transparent curtains of light flowed in waves about him in slowly changing colors. The more he moved on, the stronger the lights got until they began to dazzle with dripping globules of radiant gold.

It was altogether a fascinating place, completely unlike anything he was familiar with before. What body he had begun to vibrate in excitement, reminding him of the feeling he got when he was undergoing his final initiation into the order. He felt the joy and splendor of the moment as he forgot the weariness of the world and embraced that feeling again. He was so lost in the moment that he completely neglected everything going on around him and didn't see the figure slowly materializing before him.

"Master?" he said softly, almost frightened.

Corlieu knew the materializing shape coming through the curtains of light. It was his master, the great hero of many ages arrayed in a simple unsullied tunic. None of the pomp and flashiness of his old uniforms. Nothing to betray the fact that he looked just like anyone else.

"It's a pleasure to see you too," he said with a smile. "Don't worry, you're alright now."

"Where are we, what is this place?"

"To be certain is difficult, but we are inside of your mind."

Corlieu was taken aback a moment before continuing on.

"But I saw you dead, yet you are here in some human form. Are you some phantom of my mind?"

"I am no illusion of your dreams. I was permitted to appear to you because there is something important I need to tell you regard Axio Talphon."

"That maledicting snake!" said Corlieu, feeling his temper flare. "How could he have done such a thing?"

"I know you to still be brash and eager to settle the wrongs you see before you Nèos, but you know as one of the Axio that Talphon has greater influence over this world and superior abilities compared to us. You must awaken the nearest Axio, Fredoric Barbarossa, in order to stop him."

"Can he do it? To be sure, he's still relatively new compared to most of us in the order and Axio Talphon in particular."

"He will more than suffice. Axio Barbarossa was a great champion and is unburdened by the millennia. He has the capacity to throw him down. Now give me your dice Corlieu."

Corlieu went to pat himself down before remembering that he had no conception where or how his body was currently situated.

"How?" he said in complete confusion.

"Close your eyes and find them. They will be there if you concentrate," he said sitting down and waiting patiently.

With a deep breath, Corlieu closed his eyes and felt with his hands where his pockets ought to be. At first, it felt like his limbs were just a part of his imagination. His imagined fingers fumbled around as he tried to work with something that didn't seem to really be there. Finally, he thought he could feel the outlines of his clothes. Fingers traced the leather and cloth till he was able to recognize his belt and the pouches he had on there. Finally he was able to find the small square one that contained his dice. Almost in disbelief, certain that it was all a figment of his imagination, he undid the clasp and brought out his dice.

"Here," he said still keeping his eyes closed, not quite wanting to see if he failed or not.

A warmth engulfed his hand and he opened his eyes to see that his master had taken them. He held them up to his mouth and whispered into them and at once, they began to glow with blue light. Presently, he stopped and looked up.

"There are only six? Where are the other two?"

Corlieu grimaced and his master laughed a second.

"I see, they are not quite yours anymore. Make sure she doesn't lose them. You will need them all to find and gain access to his sanctuary. Do you remember the mountain he sleeps in?"

Corlieu nodded.

"Excellent, then you're all set."

"Wait," said Corlieu not wanting this to end so quickly. His master simply smiled and looked at him askance.

"I am not allowed to tell you what to expect when you pass on if that's what you're wondering…" he said.

"I expected not," said Corlieu. "Simply wanted to know what I'm going to do without your guidance? To be sure, you've been my instructor, guide and best friend for all this time and now I feel without direction."

At this, Corlieu's master gave the most unanticipated of reactions. He laughed and came forward, putting an arm around what felt like Corlieu's neck.

"Do you remember me before you became a member? How was I to you?"

"You always seemed to know what to do," Corlieu said simply.

"Precisely, and the secret to my confidence was simply that. Seeming to know what to do. To be truthful, I knew not the answers or what was going on around me for a majority of the time."

"You mean to say that you made it up?"

"Made it up as I went through it all. Though certainly my abilities and experiences helped mightily, I was not all knowing. Nobody in the mortal land is. Existence in the world is like that, you don't know what you're doing some of the times but you are required to take control and lead anyways."

"That doesn't strike me as impressive, or not nearly as awe inspiring as you made it seem."

"Oh, but it more impressive not knowing and doing it anyways. You've done a very fine job on your own so far if you care to know and you have the respect at least of Meliore and Corbella, even though they don't openly show it. They have learned much in a short amount of time thanks to no one but you. They still need safeguarding. Don't forget, they are still just girls in this dangerous world."

"I appreciate it master," said Corlieu feeling the burden on his shoulders lessen ever so slightly. His master walked a few steps forward and turned.

"I will be watching however. Go forth and do great things so I won't be embarrassed among the others up here when you decide to pass on as well.

Corlieu nodded and felt a grin creep across his face. It was a command, just like in the old days.

"Catch…" he said, throwing the dice at Corlieu. They flew at him gleaming blue and he reached out, feeling a surprisingly solid thunk as they hit his hands.

"THAT WAS INCREDIBLE!" came a voice.

Corlieu opened his eyes and found himself laying down with his hand outstretched. It shone blue with light streaming through his fingers. He looked to the side and saw a wide-eyed Meliore sitting up under her covers beside the young boy. They both had been eating something that now looked like it was dropped on the floor. The looks on their faces made him feel as though he was a performance.

"What happened?" he asked.

"You were laying down and hadn't moved for the longest time. I thought something was amiss so I managed to crawl over to check your breathing. After finding out how painful that was and that you were just fine despite your wounds, I came back here and left you alone for the majority of the night. A moment or two ago, you started feeling around yourself in the oddest fashion before finding those dice of yours. You held them up, threw them in the air and they glowed a vivid blue before you caught them again and woke up."

He said nothing and merely wiped his eyes. He shivered, feeling a gust of cold air wash over him. Leaves had gathered around him and he felt distinctly elderly.

"Meliore, do you have the other dice?" he asked suddenly after pocketing his.

She stuttered a second and looked away. It occurred to him that she never really knew that he was aware of her theft.

"It's okay," he said. "Indeed I've known that you've had them for a while now. I simply need to make sure you haven't lost them."

Meliore reached into her bag and felt around a moment before pulling out her hand and producing the missing two. Just like Corlieu's, they gleamed and her face was lit with the radiant.

"Let me have them back," asked Corlieu reach out.

She passed them over and a curious thing happened. The moment they left her hand and touched his, the light faded away. He looked at them in surprise and held his hand out to give them back. Upon touching her hand, they once again lit up.

"I see," he said.

"What could this mean?" she asked in amazement, picking one up and looking at it in stark curiosity.

"It means you cannot lose them," Corlieu said, standing up and stretching. "Where has Corbella gotten to?"

At this, Meliore grimaced and looked at him nervously.

"This you're not going to believe…" she said, getting to her feet slowly and helping him up.

Chapter 18

They all sat around a fire that Friar Bartal made. It was a short walk from their encampment and located in neatly concealed ditch. Though it made everything a bit more smoky than she would have liked, it did disguised the flickering flames quite nicely. Only a faint wisp of smoke belied their position, barely noticeable as it curled through the overhanging trees. For the past few minutes, the only conversation that took place was between Bartal and the boy. He spoke rapidly, in a soft tone that was almost like a whisper.

Meliore looked from side to side. To her right was Corbella, absentmindedly picking through a mushroom pasty and looking at the two of them talk. Corlieu was intently listening at Meliore's left, occasionally distracted by something in the distance and also glancing back towards their equipment up the slope.

"What are they talking about?" whispered Meliore, leaning towards Corlieu.

He opened his mouth and Meliore leaned even closed expectantly.

"No idea…" he whispered. *"I don't know enough of this language to figure it out exactly."*

"Don't be exact then," said Meliore disappointedly. *"Just, what's the subject? They've been talking for ages now."*

Corlieu sat back and blinked a few times. He stared off to the distance, causing Meliore to look off that way too. There was nothing there and she looked back and forth trying to figure out what he was gazing at before giving up and stretching her arms out.

"Well my good sir and ladies," said the Friar a moment later. "We have a most interesting thing going on here it seems. Very interesting, half believable if you don't mind me saying but I'll leave that up to yourselves to decide."

"We've been waiting forever," said Meliore, finally getting a chance to vent her frustration. "What is happening?"

"I'll tell you everything for now on one condition," he said.

"Name it," said Corlieu. "What could you possibly want?"

"I want to come with you," said the Friar. "Not only can I understand and communicate for this boy, but I have plenty of provisions and more we can collect from my monastery as we set out, plus medicines and enough skills to be of assistance."

"I think your place has already been established," said Corlieu with a nod. "Still, if you are as skillful as you say, then you are welcomed I suppose," he continued looking first at Corbella then at Meliore. Neither of them said anything, so the friar went on.

"Excellent, then this is what has been afoot with our young fellow here. He is from the east, an Empire called Nicaea. He was a… a stowaway," stuttered the friar, glancing down at the boy. He spoke to the boy a second more who then shook his head.

"Go on…" said Corlieu.

"Oh, yes. Pardon, but I wanted to ensure that he was a stowaway and not pressed into serving aboard a ship. He was running from something like an army or plague that came out of the east. It was pressing into his empire and scores of other refugees were fleeing northwards. He thought he would be safest in the west, but it seems that this army has taken some of the ships and followed him even to here. The ship landed in Marseilles where authorities captured him and mistook him for a noble because of his adornment and a ring he had stolen."

"I find that hard to believe," said Corbella. "Why would he want to draw attention to himself like that?"

"Fair point," said Corlieu. "That is hard to believe. All kingdoms have had to cope with ransoms, or the threat of them at some point in their existence."

Friar Bartal turned to the boy and the two of them spoke together for a moment more before he looked up.

"He knew that many nobles in his land get exactly what they want wherever they go and he was trying to rely on that here. I think he expected to be able to order the people of Marseilles to do exactly whatever he wanted."

"I suppose that makes sense," said Corlieu. "That was a foolish thing to do though."

Bartal shrugged

"He probably has never been outside his own land. He had no idea how dangerous such a move would be. Anyways, it worked too well and they kept him for ransom before trading him with a realm to the north. The northerners came with a large contingent and an iron carriage to take him in. At one point, he recalled hearing the sounds of fighting outside, but the carriage went on ceaselessly. He was taken to a castle and imprisoned, fed only strange cold food and waited until these two girls appeared."

The friar leaned back, taking a drink from a bladder he produced from his bags and looked at the three of them.

"That's it?" said Meliore dumbstruck with the abruptness of it all. "That can't be it, you two have been talking forever."

Friar Bartal twisted his hands a moment and looked nervously from one to the other.

"Well, you see. It took a bit longer for him to tell me because in a lot of cases, I interrupted and asked about certain points I puzzled over in a language I was trying to understand and he knows excellently."

"What language is that that you two are conversing in?" asked Corbella curiously.

"It's the modern version of the language of Hellas," said the Friar.

Corlieu nodded but Meliore and Corbella glanced at each other briefly before looking uncomprehendingly at Bartal.

"It's the language of the eastern Roman Empire," he said again.

"Greek…" said Bartal in exasperation after seeing their two blank faces again. "Honestly, who educated you two?"

Meliore and Corbella erupted in protests but a laughing Bartal calmed them down with a wave of his hand.

"I know that girls receive the bare minimum of an education in many areas," he continued on. "Even if you had more than most, I doubt your instructors ever expected that you'd come across a situation the likes of this,"

"Anyways," said Corlieu. "With that out of the way and everyone in better spirits thanks to the new guest amongst us, I do believe we have some things to discuss. Most of all, what are we going to do?"

At this point, Meliore looked up and saw a coherent plan forming in

Corlieu's mind. He closed his eyes and nodded before standing up.

"Corbella, Meliore, you two will have to forgive me for leaving out some important facts about myself. You wondered how, at my age, I could have known the things I do, seen as many battles as I have seen and be as skillful as I am. Able to outwit, outride, outmatch and outfight men of superior look. This is because I am bound to this earth as a servant of generations of humans, the same as my master before me and just like many others who exist, whether in hibernation for a long span of years or in the waking world. I have existed for just short of two millennia with a group of similar people known simply as 'The Order'. It is our job to safeguard the future of humankind and try to keep the worst of possible scenarios from coming to be."

Meliore sat flabbergasted. She had no idea how to react to his claims and her first instinct was to deny it all and call him a liar. Somehow, she just couldn't. Corlieu had truly seemed to be possessed with an uncanny degree of knowledge and experience that outclassed anyone she had ever known.

"No," said Corbella looking at him wide–eyed in disbelief. "There cannot be a way that can be true."

Her tone was curious and Meliore turned to look at her. She was half laughing but the laugh didn't reach her eyes, which stared up at Corlieu in total shock. If anything, she suddenly looked a little mad.

"I realize it is a huge amount to absorb in at once," said Corlieu holding up his hands. "If it is any consolation, this is the first time I have ever had to tell anyone about this and I've heard stories of other Order members having to fight their way out of a group of suddenly savage people who were convinced of that order member's heresy."

Corlieu looked down at the ground and laughed hard a moment. He then looked up and gave a shout. Friar Bartal and Meliore came rushing over to Corbella's side. She had fallen backwards and laid sprawled on the floor in a faint.

✶✶✶✶✶

It was now evening and the party secured their horses after travelling just shy of full speed the remainder of that day. Corbella was still reeling from the revelation Corlieu had given them earlier that day. Most of all, she was surprised how easily Bartal and Meliore had taken it. While Bartal simply shrugged when she asked him and dismissively answered *"it's certainly an interesting story,* "Meliore, in a very uncharacteristic manner, just accepted it as another strange reality of the world.

That night as they ate and Friar Bartal entertained them with stories of traveling in the wild, switching to Greek every now and then to keep the boy from feeling left out, she felt a strange uncertainty about Corlieu. He seemed to have noticed too for their moods were subdued. Finally, as they all were preparing to sleep, he came over and sat down next to a tree.

"You haven't been the same since I told you all about The Order and my true nature," he said. "The others seem to be okay with it, I mean I know not if Bartal has told the boy but if he has, then they are all fine with it. What's bothering you Corbella?"

She found herself unable to figure it out. A couple of times she made to open her mouth, but the problems she had died the instant she went to give voice to them and left her feeling unable to express herself.

"I do not know," she said. "It was always hard to believe you were as powerful as you time and time again proved yourself to be, but this is just too hard to believe. I don't know what to think."

"You are scared perhaps because you're talking to someone who has lived many multiples of times more than you have been alive?"

She nodded.

"That makes up a small part of it. If what you say is true about your order, and I have no reason to disbelieve you so far, then I feel like I'm in the presence of an ancient and incredibly powerful thing. I don't know how to act around someone like that, it is almost as though you are not wholly human."

Corlieu laughed softly and rubbed his forehead.

"All order members were normal humans at first," he said. "Just as you, Meliore, Bartal and the boy are. Many initiates try to prove themselves and fail to pass while others unsuspectingly make themselves worthy and are then accosted and admitted. But we all were normal as the everyday peasant once upon a time and living for this long does not ruin our humanity nor are we gifted with godlike powers. We are merely the culmination of human potential."

Corbella looked up at him and saw the kindness in his eyes. She nodded and relaxed for the first time that day, feeling a small wave of understanding run through her.

"If you were alive that long ago, then tell me what life was like before you became an order member."

Corlieu was silent for a while with eyes staring up to the night sky.

"The stars were the same, the exact same actually. They never seem to change and only the oldest members can swear that there has been some alteration in the way they look. I was born in the modern Papal States, in a city called Rome. In my time, it grew to be the wonder of the world and the Order safeguarded the empire that grew from it. The tall marble pillars, the decorated walls and elegant courtyards of that fair city were a wonder to behold."

As he spoke this, his face looked drawn and sad.

"What's wrong," she asked?

"I had to see that city, my home, ransacked and set afire once. It was part of our duty for it was ordained that the best course for mankind was for this to happen. I wished to never see something like that again."

For the first time, Corbella saw a flicker of the great age and burden that Corlieu bore. In living for such a tremendous length of time, he had seen many disasters that are now only history and bordering on the threshold of being myth.

"Why couldn't you do anything about it?" she asked. "What do you mean that it had to happen?"

"When an Order member reaches a point where history can diverge down one significant path or the other, they can see in their mind's eye what each path would mean to humankind and can choose the one which is best."

Corbella nodded, trying to imagine how immense a responsibility there would be with a power such as this.

"What do you see now, with this army that was besieging the castle?"

"They must be defeated," said Corlieu simply. "The alternative is the spread of disease and complete annihilation of every land they encounter."

"What do we do?" she said in alarm, sitting up with a frightened look. "Is there anything?"

"I explained to the others after you fainted that we are heading to a sanctuary in the mountains where an Axio sleeps," as he said this, he pointed off to the distance. "The Axios are something different than the rest of us Order members. They are the mighty sleeping kings from history who retire instead of die, much as we do but only awaken when their lands need them most. There is one great Axio in the isles to the north west and another who sleeps under the ruins of an old city to the far south east, and a few more. The one we are going to is Frederick Barbarossa who sleeps under a mountain just there. In the morning, it will be plain to see. He should be able to put a stop to this."

"You don't sound completely positive that he can…"

"I don't know for sure because the one he is fighting is another sleeping king from the lands far to the far northeast named Talphon. He is responsible for this army that is destroying much of these lands…."

Corlieu trailed off, not quite finishing his sentence and Corbella looked at him. She felt some dreaded expectation rising within.

"What is it?" she asked.

"…he also killed my master, the Order member that trained and initiated me. He must have that night I set out on my own. I found his sanctuary in ruins and Talphon accosted me there. I nearly did not survive, don't you remember."

Though she never met or knew Corlieu's master, she felt a huge blow land in her stomach and a wave of sadness wash over her.

"Corlieu…I'm sorry…."

"For what?" he said looking back at her. "You had no part in his demise."

"I realize that, but…" she said, not knowing what to say.

"…but you morn for the sadness it is causing me and it makes you fear for the loss of people just as important to you?" he said, continuing for her.

"You know, you do have an annoyingly accurate way with words…"

They both laughed lightly and Corbella relaxed even more so. There was nothing different from the Corlieu she knew before. The revelation of his long past changed nothing about him. He was as normal a human as could be hoped for. Presently, he stopped laughing.

"Watch this…" he whispered reaching behind him and unsheathing the great sword. He winked and turned it flat before lightly slapping it atop a bush behind him. Instead of the sound of breaking twigs, she heard a cry of pain.

"You can come out you three," said Corlieu. "No need to hide and creep around the bushes."

Friar Bartal popped his head up, followed closely by the boy and Meliore who was rubbing her forehead.

"You could have just asked you know," grumbled Meliore.

They all broke out laughing, including Meliore when the ridiculousness of the moment dawned upon her.

"So, that's who we have to defeat," said Bartal once they stopped laughing. "This…Talphon fellow is responsible for the death and disease."

"And he's after us as well," said Corlieu.

"By us, do you mean…" started Meliore looking at Corbella and Bartal.

"No, no," said Corlieu. "You two are relatively safe from his direct wrath unless you happen to get in the way. No, he is personally after this boy here and any member of the Order he can get his hands on, which means me."

"So the sooner we awaken this Barbarossa, the sooner we are able to set everything right?" asked Corbella.

"Exactly," said Corlieu. "I recommend we get some sleep now. Stay hidden if anything happens and if a mist covers us in the night which very well might happen, stay still and cover your face."

"Do you mean," asked Meliore looking around nervously, "that they are around here?"

"Yes," said Corlieu. "I did say that they are looking for us didn't I?"

They all spread out and prepared to sleep. Corbella however was unable to find anywhere comfortable and just nestled down next to Meliore.

"Try sleeping with that on your mind…" Meliore said thoroughly agitated and glancing from side to side. "Do you wager that they'll get us while the moon is up or after it goes down?"

"I don't know what you're talking about," said Corbella. "We've got Corlieu. He knows what to do."

"He could have left that part about being chased out though. It's hard enough trying to rest without imagining shapes crawling out of the shadows around us."

"You'll see," said Corbella, dozing off to sleep. "We'll be okay. It's Corlieu and the boy that they want. We're safe as long as we maintain our impeccable beauty."

"Good heavens," shrieked Meliore sitting straight up. "Do you realize how long it has been since we have washed ourselves or even combed our hair?"

"I haven't even thought about that," said Corbella. "I suppose you do get used to the constant grimy feeling. Still though, I have a suspicion that everything will be alright."

Chapter 19

Another whole day of riding. Non–stop without even a second or two of rest and a short nap at night. Never have I ridden so much in my life and we're expected to go on again this entire day!

Every bone and muscle in Meliore's body ached and still Corlieu guided them forward. The urgency in his voice was very real and growing with every passing moment. His typically fiery horse now hung its head low and merely seemed mischievous instead of looking as though it was actively plotting against him. Friar Bartal's large horse still managed to keep up the pace as well, but whenever they slowed she could see it taking deep panting breaths. She had no idea what her horse looked like, but she was certain that he was no different.

They were a beaten, disheveled mess when Corlieu finally halted them and dismounted. At this point, the mountain had grown huge and threatening, but the lands around it seemed peaceful. She felt as though she could easily spend a few days, enjoying the scenery and walking there without a care in the world. Only her suspicion, partially enflamed by Corlieu's agitation, told her that there was danger all around them.

"We should probably rest and gather some strength here," he said tying up his horse.

They all dismounted and followed his lead. Pulling out some food and taking a seat, Meliore heard Corbella groan as she stretched out her legs and massaged her knees. For a moment, they sat in silence and ate. Each were lost in their own thoughts until Corlieu, finishing his food, got up and looked at them all.

"It is a certain thing that Talphon and the army is waiting for us around the mountain. I was hoping to reach it before they did, but I am now certain that the way is held against us. The only hope we have is to sneak past and find the entrance. There's a small chance that we'll be lucky for I little expect them to think we're so close. Stay with me and once I find the way in we will be safe."

"How are we going to be safe?" asked Meliore curiously.

"The entrance is made to look like a side of the mountain. Typically, it is a side of the mountain unless you possess a way in," said Corlieu, reaching into his pocket and producing his set of dice. "You still have the two I entrusted to you, Meliore…" he said, looking expectantly at her.

"Yes, I have them right here," she said pulling them out of a pouch.

"Then we are ready to go. When we draw near to the mountain, pull out your dice and take note of the color. They should get brighter the closer you get to the entrance and I believe they give some type of indication when you are there and able to enter."

"Should? Believe? It sounds like you haven't done this thing before," said Corbella suspiciously.

"No, I actually haven't," said Corlieu as he put his dice back. "I have never been in this sanctuary to be honest, only told of it and don't fully know what to expect once we are inside."

Meliore didn't feel reassured and by the look Corbella was giving her, neither did she. The friar on the other hand simply slapped his legs, stood up and looked around at them.

"Then, I think it's time for us to get moving?"

"Now? Already?" said Meliore tensing up. "Can't we just wait a little more?"

"For what?" asked Bartal with a grim laugh. "There is nothing to be had now except to go. Waiting I fear won't make our lot any easier."

"Indeed it will not," said Corlieu. "Our only hope now is in speed and stealth."

Meliore crammed one more pasty into her mouth and followed Corbella to their horse. Soon, they were setting off at a walk towards the mountain. Every now and then, Corlieu would take out his dice and look appraisingly at them. Meliore did the same, but upon seeing nothing she replaced them in her bag.

They walked, avoiding the open plains and stayed down as low as they could manage. Still, with the noonday sun reaching its apex, they were hard pressed to remain unseen. At one point, Corlieu stopped, holding out his hand to stop the others immediately.

"What is it?" whispered Bartal.

"There is something there…" said Corlieu, pointing down a ravine.

Meliore strained her eyes but couldn't see anything. They remained in that spot, unmoving for a few minutes while she scanned back and forth. Foliage and trees, bushes and stones littered the area but there was nothing....

"I see something!" Corbella gasped.

"Where?" asked Meliore.

Corlieu twisted his head and looked at them angrily and they both shut their mouths. Corbella pointed over Meliore's shoulder and down a ravine. She took a sharp intake of breath as she saw them, a group of figures skirted around the shadows of the trees. They weaved in and out, over and around leaving a thin trail of mist behind them.

None of them moved. The urgent stillness of the situation was so complete that the horses did not even flick their ears. They simply waited while the flittering figures made their way deeper into the forest. Slowly, of them stopped and put his head close to the ground as though it was listening.

"Oh no..." said Corlieu, moving his horse a step or two away from the creatures.

It seemed to be slow motion, but as the creature raised its head, it stared directly at Meliore and let off a loud yell.

"RUN!" shouted Corlieu.

At once all three of their horses sprang into action. Meliore hastily grabbed mane as her horse's speed drove her backwards, against Corbella. Corlieu led them through the woods and up a hill. All at once, on the other side there erupted a group of other riders. They made straight for Corlieu and Bartal, in effect cutting the girls off from them in one surprisingly quick motion.

"CORLIEU!" yelled Corbella as Meliore steered into the clearing and felt her horse pick up speed.

"HEAD TO THE MOUNTAIN!" he yelled before passing out of sight with a host of mist spewing riders behind him.

Why does this always seem to happen to us?

Meliore held onto her horse's mane and gripped with her leg as she felt him go bounding over a small stream. Corbella's arms tightened around her waist and she heard her cousin take in a big gulp of air as the landing knocked her head into Meliore's back.

"PLEASE RESTRAIN ANY DESIRE TO KILL ME TODAY!" Corbella yelled.

"IT'S NOT ME YOU SHOULD BE WORRYING ABOUT!" yelled Meliore taking a glance behind her.

A small group of mounted black shapes were holding the distance between them. So long as they kept it up, they should not get caught but if something happened to their horse or if one of them fell then they would be overtaken.

Stocatta tried as hard as he might, sensing Meliore's fear and having the decency to not try throwing them off and running free. He picked his footing as carefully as speed allowed and tore into the open when the ground was flat. It was not enough however, the shapes behind them came unceasingly on. They seemed unaffected by fatigue and continued on their rapacious chase.

A line of trees came up and ended. Meliore pushed herself up a little bit and looked around at a vast green plain peppered with yellow flowers and white tufts. They were heading diagonally away from the mountainside now, and she made to correct their direction when a large group burst from the tree line some distance to their left. It was Corlieu in the lead with Bartal and the boy holding on just behind him. A large following of the black army rode after them and at its front was a great shape.

All at once, the lead figure in the army pursuing Corlieu looked over towards Meliore. She could see the face, even from this far off and his mouth opened. An ear splitting sound crossed the valley and she felt her horse shy away and stumble a moment. She sat back, squashing Corbella for a moment and squeezed the horse forward still. He recovered his footing and went one.

"WHAT IN PETER'S NAME WAS THAT?" yelled Corbella.

"HEAVEN KNOWS, IT CAME FROM THE OTHER GROUP OF PURSUERS," she said looking around at the mounted riders behind her.

"MELIORE! THEY'RE TURNING ASIDE!"

Sure enough, Meliore turned around and looked. They both stared in a combination of relief and horror as the group chasing after them turned sharply off and headed towards Corlieu. At the angle they were going, they would be able to cut him off from the mountain.

"CORLIEU!" yelled Corbella, waving a hand frantically.

Somehow, despite the noise of their galloping horses, the din of the chasing army and distance, Corlieu looked up and saw the new group coming to cut them off. Maybe Corbella's yell was unnecessary and he would have looked up anyways, but Meliore breathed a sigh of relief as Corlieu led Bartal away from the oncoming group.

She let her horse slow down significantly and they trotted far to the right, into the tree line. Meliore and Corbella were so attentive to the chase on the other side of the valley that they weren't paying attention to where their horse was going. Steady, it slowed its trot into a walk and before Meliore knew what happened, the horse had pitched forward and she found herself suddenly rolling off one side and landing painfully on a cursing Corbella.

Meliore got to her feet quickly, not wanting to miss what happened. Despite her loss of height, she could just barely see as Bartal and Corlieu made it to the tree line and disappeared ahead of both pursuing groups.

"THEY MADE IT!" she yelled in joy, turning around and helping Corbella up. *"THEY'LL MAKE IT TO THE MOUNTAIN YET, THAT CORLIEU AND HIS MEAN LITTLE HORSE CAN DO ANYTHING!"*

"And what shalt we do about our miserable beast?" Corbella said, looking behind Meliore with a grimace on her face.

Their horse had ditched them at the edge of a shallow pool and was rolling around in the muddy water. All their bags were filthy and his chestnut coat was blackened.

"What about our bags?" said Meliore in alarm, rushing over to try and get him up.

"There's hardly anything that's really breakable in there and Bartal had all our food aside from a few of my biscuits. Our clothes are buckled away and should stay relatively alright."

"But still…" she said, trailing off and looking at the horse feeling deflated. It stood up now, soaked and caked in mud but looking mildly pleased. After stretching one of the hind legs, it walked over to some grass and started grazing.

"I haven't a clue what you're going to do but I think we should change," said Corbella.

"Why and out of all the times why now?"

"Think a moment, the army has gone off after Bartal, Corlieu and the boy for now so we're not likely to suffer another chase. There's a fair chance that if we do run into them, they would ne'er pass up the likelihood of capturing us since we have been a part of the group. If we are boys again however…."

Meliore hung her head and assented that she had a point. It made decent sense for them to once again don their familiar disguises before heading towards the mountain. She just didn't know how she could once again suffer through having her hair pinned up and shoved into her hat.

"Mayst we eat first?" she asked with a sigh. "A biscuit if you please! I'll eat while I tie up your hair."

Over the next few moments, Meliore struggled as she worked on Corbella's hair. The fact that they hadn't bathed in what felt like ages made their hair difficult to braid and shape. As a result, Meliore could never get rid of all the strands sticking out under Corbella's hat. She crammed a biscuit into her mouth angrily before spitting a little of it out and looking at it suspiciously.

"Something is more than a little amiss with these biscuits. I don't know why but it doesn't taste like water!"

Corbella's biscuits had been flattened and wet from Stocatta's rolling but none of the mud or water had soaked into them. Neither of them could understand why they were damp and reasoned that her drinking water must have leaked when their horse rolled.

"I can't help it, I don't know but it seems to taste alright to me," said Corbella. "If anything better," she said sampling a morsel and thinking perplexedly at the sweet flavor it suddenly had.

They had spent the next few minutes dressing themselves. Stocatta still grazed, completely oblivious to them and there hadn't been any signs of anyone else the entire time. In fact, aside from worrying about the others, the only other thing that bothered them was the explanation for the change in their food.

"All right," came a deep strong voice. "I'm vested up and ready, are you done yet?"

Meliore jumped and turned around sharply, looking around and then staring at Corbella hesitantly.

"Care to say that again?" she asked.

"I only asked if you were ready?" Corbella said again in an absurdly deep voice.

Meliore laughed, unable to help herself and rolled backwards onto the ground.

"What?" Corbella angrily asked.

"You sound just like Gennaro, except maybe a little deeper. What happened to your voice? You sound ridiculous!"

As she said this, Meliore heard her voice growing deeper and stopped suddenly. She smacked her lips and spoke a few words, slowly. She could feel uncharacteristically deep vibrations run through her body with each word. As she kept playing around, trying to make her voice return to its normal pitch, a laughing Corbella perked up and ran over to her bags.

"Com'ere," she said. "I am thinking I perhaps found the source of our damp biscuits..."

Meliore came running over, still rubbing her throat and looked into Corbella's bag. There was a small wet pouch that was cut up from a collection of broken glass inside.

"What's that?"

"Don't you remember that vial I purchased in Genoa? The one from that old shopkeeper you bought the little statue from right before we met Gennaro?"

They both stared down at the pouch of broken glass dumbfounded.

"So what you are telling me," Meliore started, "is that vial was in there."

Corbella nodded.

"…and it broken when your horse rolled?"

Again she nodded.

"…and we ate biscuits that were soggy with… *WHATEVER THAT WAS?!*"

"I would wager that's what happened," said Corbella casting the broken glass aside and grunting in her deep voice. "That fellow did say that it would make me someone other than myself, or something like that."

They both absentmindedly felt their throats and were making repeated attempts at correcting their pitch. It was no luck though, and neither of them could even get close to their former voices.

"Do you think it is permanent?" asked Meliore.

Corbella opened her mouth to respond but was cut short by another loud voice from across the valley.

"THERE THEY ARE!"

Meliore turned and saw in fright that the army had returned and arrayed itself along the whole side of the valley. They were now coming at a great speed and also were sending up great echoing shouts. Responding shouts came from all around them and Meliore whirled around, listening to the noise in rapidly growing concern.

"Why are they coming after us…?" asked Meliore, walking backwards and staring at the oncoming army in growing fright.

"QUICK!" yelled Corbella picking up her bag. *"WHERE'S STOCATTA?"*

Thankfully, Meliore's horse had remained nearby and did not flee as the ground shook from the oncoming army. It looked ready to however and no sooner did they both scurry on did it then bolt off into the nearby woods. Meliore kicked herself for not taking advantage of the time they had to head towards the mountain.

"WHAT DO WE DO?" screamed Meliore over the sound of the onrushing wind. *"IF THEY'RE CHASING US, THEN THAT MUST MEAN THAT THEY CAUGHT THE OTHERS."*

"I CAN'T TELL FOR SURE. THE WAY THEY IGNORED US BEFORE AND CHASED AFTER THE OTHERS MAKES ME THINK THEY DIDN'T CARE ABOUT US ONE BIT. THEY ONLY WANTED…."

Corbella's voice trailed off and she looked back at Meliore, then down at her horse.

"MAYBE THEY THINK WE'RE BARTAL AND THE BOY?"

"WHAT, THAT'S INCOMPREHENSIBLE! NO WAY WOULD THEY COULD DO THAT!"

"THINK ABOUT IT. WE LOOK LIKE TWO MEN, ON A HORSE THAT NOW LOOKS LIKE ONE OF THE OTHER'S HORSES. OF COURSE

WE'RE THEM AND THEY'RE COMING FOR US. HEAVEN KNOWS WHAT WILL HAPPEN SHOULD THEY FIND OUT THEIR MISTAKE!"

Meliore rested her head against Corbella's back. Unfortunately it made just enough sense to be believable. With their clothing, deep voices and dirty horse, it was possible that was the case. If so, then the others were still alive and had given the army the slip.

"TO THE MOUNTAIN?" she yelled to Corbella.

"YES, I REMEMBER WHERE CORLIEU SAID THE ENTRANCE WAS. WE'LL MAKE IT!" Meliore said, slapping her side and feeling the dice.

At that, fresh shouts and sounds of trumpets echoed around them and Meliore saw the woods come to life with shapes. She shouted and squeezed eyes shut and tightened her arms around Corbella.

"I BET THEY THINK YOU'RE THE PRINCE," she said, shaking in fright.

She didn't even bother paying attention to what Corbella said. They needed to make it to the mountain.

Chapter 20

Corlieu rode on, pressing his horse up the mountainside. It was hard to believe, but the only living things he saw were occasionally scattering wildlife. Scarcely a moment before, the world around them was weaved in the mists of the army and faint forms were seen sometimes too close and other times not far enough away. It was never certain if they could have remained hidden for much longer, so Corlieu was slowly preparing Bartal and the boy to make another run for it when he saw one of the shades suddenly tense up and look back in the direction of the valley. It tore off with an awful clamor in that direction followed by many more leaving only a slowly dissipating mist.

"They are all gone! Corlieu, do you know the reason?" yelled Bartal from behind.

"I have suspicions. They might have gone ahead of us to simply block the way up or lay in ambush."

"But you doubt this?" he responded after a moment and went to say something else but stopped suddenly. Corlieu turned and saw that the boy was saying something in his ear.

"He wants to know what about the two girls? He says they did save him from his imprisonment after all."

"They should be all right. It's us they want. They had a good amount of time to escape on their own by now or make their way into the mountain. As for what happened to the army, I don't believe they're lying in ambush. We would know because of the mists."

In the back of his mind, Corlieu struggled to understand what would draw the entire force off like that. Talphon had only two objectives: capturing himself and the boy. Bartal and the girls could walk away relatively untroubled, even now.

Corlieu shook his head and concentrated on where he was going. None of it really made sense and he needed to ensure he didn't miss the entrance. He pulled out his dice as they neared a steep edge of the mountain and he saw them begin to glow with life. Step by step they crept and the light amplified until it gave off a flash and went dark.

"This is it," he said with a look of relief. "Follow as close as you dare, our horses might take fright at first."

They walked straight into the mountainside and the stone melted away. Corlieu's horse scurried to one side and snorted wildly, looking around in shock. He spent a minute there, scratching the animal's mane and waiting for it to relax. They were in a stone hallway climbing steeply up and gently curving to the right. Quickly they ascended the unchanging hall, seeing nothing and feeling as though it stretched on for uncounted hours.

Finally, as Corlieu was growing impatient and was going to canter, there was a change. The earthy smell of the hall gave way to fresh air and an arch appeared.

"By the heavens above…" said Bartal as they rode through it.

Corlieu said nothing, but those same words passed through his mind. They were now at a high cliff of the mountain, looking down upon the entire countryside. The mists of the army were gathered all about the lands below them right up into the foot of the mountain and from this vantage point, Corlieu could see how great it had become. The forms of soldiers and the spread of their destruction was evident. Even as he looked, it seemed like the green forests were turning brown before his eyes and the land was growing murky.

"What now?" said Bartal.

Walking away from the cliff, Corlieu again pulled out his dice hoping for another flash indicating where he was supposed to go. Nothing of the sort happened, however, and he wandered this way and that, seeing no change in the color.

"*CORBOLLA,*" said a very strange voice.

"What did he say?" said Corlieu, spinning around and seeing the boy pointing down the hallway they came up.

"*…EEENIN CORBOLLA,*" he said again looking down the hallway.

"*Dear me!*" shouted the Friar jumping to his feet. "*He's saying it's Corbella!*"

Corlieu heard the sound of galloping hooves and realized what was happening just soon enough to rush forward. A muddy, foaming horse came running up and he barely managed to grab the reins and help slow it down. It and its two passengers were wild and staring around desperately.

"*THEY'RE STILL BEHIND US!*" yelled Meliore in an absurdly basso—

profundo voice, jumping off the horse with Corbella and making a frantic run in a circle before realizing there was no place to hide. *"I SWEAR, THEY WERE THIS CLOSE EVERY STEP OF THE WAY!"*

"NO, NO," said Corbella, also in a very bizarre and deep voice. *"WE JUST MANAGED TO LOSE THEM WHEN WE VANISHED INTO THE MOUNTAINSIDE, IT'S OKAY!"*

Corbella was just starting to stand up when Meliore saw her, ran over and tackled her.

"ON THE GROUND! WHAT—ARE YOU TYRYING TO GIVE OUR POSITION AWAY!?"

She leapt up and started dragging a vehemently cursing Corbella around by the collar. Corlieu watched all this in slight amusement but was busy with their horse, which, in its present condition, might go running off the cliff. The girls were okay, as far as he knew. They were dirty and covered in leaves and scratches. A large, though shallow gash went down Meliore's back and Corbella's lip was bloody.

"BARTAL," yelled Corlieu. *"WILL YOU DO SOMETHING ABOUT THOSE TWO?"*

The friar was already rummaging around his bags, shaking his head and looking from one corner to the other.

"I suppose there's nothing for it," he said with a sour expression. He grabbed a large bladder and walked over to the girls before emptying the contents suddenly on them. They both stopped, mid–argument and blinked looking around.

"Bartal! What did you do that for?" they both said.

"Because your heads were half off and I wish I hadn't, that was the last of my mead! Look at you two, what on earth happened and how can you possibly speak in such deep voices?"

"It was this vial I bought in Genoa," said Corbella, getting up and straightening herself out in a slightly disoriented fashion. "It got into some food we ate and it made our voices like this. For some reason, the army started chasing after us and we've been on the run the whole time."

"The dice, Corlieu," shouted Meliore. "In my hands they started to glow just like you said! We were practically crashing against the rocks when they flashed and we went into the wall. I don't believe we escaped! Oh, I wish I could have seen their faces when we vanished."

Corlieu at this point had calmed their horse down and tied it alongside the others. He pulled the saddle and equipment off, watched as they made noises and bit each other, and then were cowed enough to settle down to eating grass. He walked over to the cliff and looked out upon the valley. The army surely was gathered below them. They had all the advantage and Corlieu had none. Numbers, time and the need for supplies were all against them.

"Even more so now," Corlieu whispered in dread, seeing the glint of dim sunlight off of more incoming arms in the distance. Against an army that big, they had no chance. Axio or not.

He turned, not wanting to dwell any longer on the disappointing though to find Bartal handing the girls a small glass each.

"…a most curious malady of the throat that is," he was saying. "It does not suit young ladies such as yourselves to have voices that might bring the snows high above crashing down upon our heads. Try this, it should return you to your proper sounds."

The two girls quickly downed the drinks before looks of disgust crossed their faces.

"What was in there?" asked Corbella, stifling a gigantic burp and instead hissing like a kettle. "That was the most awful thing I have ever tasted in my life!"

"It is probably better that you know not," said Bartal wringing his hands. "It is a type of ground up fish though, along with plant matter."

"And you carry this around all the time?" asked Meliore. "I don't feel anything either, is my voice changing yet?"

"You sound just as horrible as ever," said Corbella, suddenly in her normal voice.

"You rotten, accursed…!" started Meliore, also in a voice that had suddenly changed back to normal.

"ENOUGH!" said Corlieu, and they both stopped. "Meliore, it's now time. Hand me your dice."

She got up and rummaged through her pouches. For one instant, he twitched in horror as he imagined her showing him empty pockets with a shrug, but it passed when she gave a look of triumph and came running over with them in hand.

All together again, the dice now gleamed and pulsed slowly. They rejoiced, radiating internal light that emblazoned every edge and gilded carving. He walked to the mountainside and he saw them flash just as before. The mountainside melted away and before them was a tall gaping entrance. A figure came running over excitedly and bowed hurriedly before them.

Chapter 21

"Greetings, my name is Alexandra and I am the Arger of this sanctuary. It's been a long time since we have had any visitors."

"I wonder why…" whispered Corbella.

"Excuse us," said Corlieu quickly. "We are extremely pressed at the moment."

"…because of the army, and Axio Talphon and the rest of the surrounding events?" Alexandra said as easily as though she was reciting poem.

"How in the heavens do you know that?" asked Meliore, pushing past Corlieu and looking at her in amazement.

Alexandra laughed and motioned them all inside. She walked briskly down the torch lit hallways and motioned them after her. Two others dressed in a similar fashion came running up.

"There are three horses outside, do bring them in and take them down to the livery," she said. They nodded and set off for the entrance without a word.

"Back to your question, we Argers might live in mountains but we are not hermits. News from the lesser sanctuary members reaches us, along with supplies. You don't think we eat stones do you?"

"Ah me, no that wasn't at all what I meant," Meliore mumbled. "All of this only happened within the past month and nobody hears of anything that fast."

"If you are curious, then don't be. The reality is that we know what's been going on and other members in the east have been at work."

Corlieu paused a moment to think about that.

"The other members have been working on this too? What have they done? It's seemed that we've been on our own this whole time."

"You know that Order members operate in independent groups, so what has exactly been afoot is unknown to us. We have had some forewarning though, but that's beside the point. Right now, the most pressing thing is to awaken Axio Barbarossa. Follow me!"

They walked around a corner and into a vast chamber. It was Corlieu's first time in the sanctuary of Barbarossa and he drew in a breath at the majesty of it. Along the wall were large statues carven into the stone. They were adorned with cylindrical helmets and thin rectangular eyeholes fashioned in such a way as to look like crosses. Before them, they presented large bearded axes as though they were greeting a king. Light from the torches danced along the walls, silhouetting the great stone shapes, and yet their presence was not menacing. The orange light gave them a noble look and their vestments were elegantly detailed in shimmering silvers and gold. It was in all, an awe–inspiring place.

Presently, they crossed the entirety of the hall and came to the far wall where a door stood.

"Corlieu..." whispered Corbella in a frightened voice. *"The statues...they're looking at us...."*

He spun around and gaped.

Were all of them looking in this direction before? No, but I can't be sure. They might have been....

"The statues are awakening," said Alexandra. "My mentor, the former Arger, told me that this would happen when Axio Barbarossa is needed and ought to be awakened. If they are moving however...."

As she said this, the statues lowered their axes and stepped out from the walls. They assembled in a large semi–circle around the party and rested the axe heads against the ground. There they stood, waiting expectantly it seemed.

"Now that that is done," Alexandra continued, "we need to wait on our dear Robert Corlieu here to awaken him."

"Your name is Robert?" asked Corbella with a snicker.

"Don't make me separate your tongue from the rest of you," he said with a gulp, staring at the door dumbfounded.

"Fair enough, no pressure Robert."

Corlieu walked up to the door and ran his hands over it. Stone is hard to work with at the best of times, but such a large door as this was baffling. The alternating roughly and painstakingly carved portions hid any indication of seams, cracks, hinges or anything that wasn't decorative. He still had his dice in his right hand and held them aloft. They glowed with that same soft blue light he remembered and he walked around the doorway as they changed in intensity. Towards one section, they suddenly gleamed gold and gave off a brilliant flash that dazzled his eyes.

In his blindness, he heard gasps and excitement coming from behind him. He rubbed his eyes quickly, but it took a moment for them to regain their normal functioning capacity. When they did, he saw a greatly muscled figure standing before him.

"EDELFREI! " said the figure, coming forward and embracing Corlieu. He recoiled slightly because not only was Barbarossa prodigiously strong, but he also smelled terribly of vinegar.

"I'm honored by your presence, Axio," he said trying to hold his breath. Something of his discomfort must have been apparent because Barbarossa let go and looked at him a moment.

"You look disturbed," he said after glancing him up and down. "I trust that the Arger here has made you comfortable upon your arrival?"

From within the group, Alexandra gave a cough and stepped forward.

"I'm afraid there hasn't been time for that," she started. "As we speak, Axio Talphon is holding the mountain against us. We have the means to resist for a while, but this sanctuary was not build to withstand an earnest assault or a siege. Particularly since Talphon would know this place's weaknesses."

Axio Barbarossa straightened up and looked out, over the group. He closed his eyes and took in a deep breath for a moment before looking back at Corlieu.

"So my land and people need me?"

"Yes," responded Corlieu.

"Let us go see what is before us then," he said, striding through the group. He stopped short when he got to Meliore and Corbella though. He glanced down at them with pursed lips.

"What brings these two ladies to my abode?" he said turning to Corlieu. "They certainly haven't the look of those that maintain the sanctuary. They aren't Order members either or great warriors to aid us in our situation."

"They have aided me along the way," said Corlieu nervously. He didn't expect

Barbarossa to notice or care and was at a loss at what to say. "Though they are young, they have done well and have learnt how to fight from me."

"Show me," he said. "Draw your weapons!"

Meliore and Corbella looked frighteningly at each other before reaching for where their sticks Corlieu had cut for them used to be. They felt their pockets and blank looks crossed their faces before they held up their fists.

Barbarossa stared at them for full ten seconds before bursting out in laughter. He pointed at one of his knights and spoke in an unknown language before continuing down the hallway. Corlieu went to follow him but was stopped by Meliore.

"What's going to happen to us?" she asked.

"I think he sent for someone to get you two properly equipped," he said with a grin. "You'll need more to fight with than just fists."

"YOU MEAN WE'RE GOING TO FIGHT?" Corbella said in shock.

"What on earth do you think we were going to have to do, curse at them from up here?" asked an exasperated Corlieu.

"It's just… I…" started Corbella looking nervous.

"It is real combat Corlieu!" shouted Meliore.

Corlieu started walking down the hallways after Barbarossa.

"In case you two haven't noticed," he shouted over his shoulder, "you've already been through a number of fights already. Just wait there and the knight will help you."

Axio Barbarossa was already at the cliff that marked the entrance to his sanctuary when Corlieu reached him. His knights were assembled around, staring out upon the land and the mists that were building below.

"You have been fortunate," he said to Corlieu after a moment. "How you were able to evade Talphon and the pestilence they have been spreading is beyond me. Already, I can feel the land and people growing sick and dying in droves. Many more have perished around the old Roman sea as well."

He turned to Corlieu a moment and his face was drawn and saddened.

"It pains me, especially knowing that it has spread to my homeland as well.

This is not the only army that is threatening the whole of this land, but it is the most important. Should we defeat Axio Talphon, then the others will wither and the disease will fade away into memory."

"Can we defeat him? Seven of us and your knights against an army of thousands…" asked Corlieu uncertainly.

At this, Barbarossa sent up a might laugh and clapped Corlieu on the shoulder.

"Look!" he said, steering Corlieu's eyes over in the distance.

Again, he saw the glitter of the fading sunlight off armor and weapons. He looked from Barbarossa to them and back again.

"Are they not more of our besiegers?"

"No, indeed they are not," said Barbarossa. "It is something else. Another army that has come to us in our need!"

"How is this possible?" said Corlieu, realizing for the first time that they really were an army of living men. "To come at just such a time as this is almost an act of the heavens!"

"You know as well as I do that the Order has many allies. Certainly some of our brethren have steered them hither, if they are not in fact amongst them."

Corlieu stood silently a moment. He was once again reminded of how formidable a machine the Order could be in a pinch. Only a span of weeks ago, he was desperate and his mission was in disarray. Now he had succeeded in tracking and evading Talphon and the army, leading them to the mountain where Barbarossa was awakened and with the help of the incoming army, could put an end to his treachery.

"I know what you're thinking," Barbarossa said looking at Corlieu. "It has been a long journey for you peppered with pain and sadness, great joy and treasure that never was meant to be. You have done well Edelfrei and your master knows this as well."

"Thank you," he said nodding his head. "I just wish that he was here."

"It was the will of the heavens, you cannot fight that. He knows it and so do you, though the pain makes it uncomfortable to admit. You now have others that look up to you now and you must guide them as your master did with you."

Behind him, Corlieu heard shouting and turned to see Meliore and Corbella getting pushed through the entrance by the knight and Alexandra.

"They were trying to hide!" Alexandra said in irritation. "I cannot believe they would attempt such a thing, at a time like this."

"Look at this thing," said Corbella, holding up her sword. It was thin and of moderate length. "What am I supposed to do with this, stick frogs?" Behind her, Meliore heaved up a crossbow and held it awkwardly in her arms. She went to say something, but was interrupted.

"By the grace of the heavens," said Alexandra irritably. "Here, let me show you what you do with these…."

They then devolved into a rumble of arguments and quick instructions, joined by the friar who came up, armed with a spear and towing the boy behind him. A moment passed before the boy went running up excitedly and pointed to the oncoming army, yelling in excitement.

"What is he saying?" asked Corlieu.

"He said that that army is Byzantinian and they have the banner of his… um… royal house."

At that, Corbella and Meliore stopped their fighting and looked at Bartal in shock.

"He's royalty?" asked Meliore.

"He expressly asked that I not mention it," said Bartal quickly. "He was concerned that he would be subject to ransom again and though I disagreed, I honored his wish."

"CAN YOU TWO PAY ATTENTION FOR JUST A MOMENT!" shouted an exasperated Alexandra. *"I AM TRYING TO HELP YOU TWO STAY ALIVE AFTERALL!"*

"No time for it Arger," said Barbarossa holding up a hand. "We must now go down to meet our besiegers."

"But we're not ready, what do we do?" asked Corbella nervously.

"You will fight because it is what you must do," he responded. One of his knights came forward and presented him with a great sword and shield adorned with the cross. Another knelt before him and held aloft a crown. Alexandra gave off a gasp and rushed forward to place the crown on his head.

"We will be victorious young one," he said to Corbella. "We have an army and you are surrounded by many warriors who are worth thrice their weight in numbers of soldiers. Though this be your first taste of a real battle, come and do not be afraid."

Chapter 22

Corbella was pushed through the solid looking entrance by one of the knights and out into the land surrounding the mountain. Beside her, Meliore clutched at her crossbow and looked around nervously. Barbarossa and Corlieu were assembled in a group in front of them along with Alexandra, who was holding in her hands an elegantly curved blade. The massive forms of the knights stood on their flanks.

Surrounding them, however, was the army, and facing Barbarossa and Corlieu was none other than Axio Talphon himself. He laughed when he saw them all come forward.

"What sort of a party is this?" he said mockingly. "Certainly not a force to try and contend with me?"

"BE SILENT BETRAYER!" shouted Corlieu, unsheathing his sword and holding it aloft. *"I HAVE NO INTENTION OF TRADING ANYTHING LESS THAN YOUR LIFE FOR RETRIBUTION."*

"Spare me your indignation young one," said Talphon. "You have been able to evade us by fortune and good luck so far, but now you are at the end of your rope and death is upon all who stand here."

The army closed in a few steps and Barbarossa's knights held their axes at the ready, but still the attack did not come.

"What is the matter?" asked Barbarossa curiously, walking a step toward Talphon who straightened up as though he was struck on the nose. "I have known you for quite an extended length of time as we fought together in the holy wars. This is not like you, what has happened since we last bid farewell as friends?"

"Nothing has happened to me," Axio Talphon replied venomously. "I have seen the truth of this world and the petty job we have been tasked to perform in it for these people. If we ever wish to succeed in our mission, we must bear the burden of greater control and power."

"That is not our calling," said Barbarossa sternly. "In forfeiting our mission, you have turned yourself against the Order and the way of all things in this world. There is no choice for us now!"

With those words, Barbarossa and Corlieu flung themselves at Talphon. In a flurry of movement, the clash of weapons echoed against the mountainside like a thunder crack. From all sides, the forces pressed down upon them and the knights began swinging their great axes.

It was then that everything around Corbella turned to chaos.

"We're surrounded!" she heard Meliore shriek. "What do we do?"

"It seems as though we are," said Bartal, holding the Prince back with one hand and holding a spear at the ready with the other.

"Good," said Alexandra at their side, striking out at an enemy that had weaved its way past one of the knights. "In that case, attack in every direction!"

Corbella looked around at the incredible clamor of battle. They were somewhat protected, as the knights made a solid wall around them and were swinging their axes in great spiraling patters. However, they were slowly getting pushed in and unless they did something, the army would press them together in a knot from which there would be no room to fight.

"What do we do?" she asked, looking at Meliore who was hastily trying to wind up her crossbow like Alexandra had just taught her when a figure dodged through one of the axe strokes and swooped upon her for the kill.

"MELIORE!" Corbella cried, leaping forward with sword in hand and just managing to thrust its tip into the oncoming attacker. It screamed in pain and crumpled backwards.

She looked at her sword in amazement. It was frighteningly easier to use than she thought it would have been. The thrust had penetrated whatever armor was around the attacker's chest and left a gaping entrance hole. There was barely time for reflection before her attention was drawn back to the battle around her.

The circle of knights was closing in around them and Alexandra and Friar Bartal were fighting like mad. Meliore had figured out the crossbow and was slowly shooting bolts into the enemy lines. It was not enough, however, and one of the knights was overwhelmed and toppled over in front of Corbella. Before she knew it, she was face–to–face with a number of foes.

There was no time to think about what she was doing, and by some grace of the heavens Corbella did not panic and run. Instead, she held her sword aloft like Corlieu had shown her and intercepted the first strike and dodged the second. A third, aimed directly for her head, never completed its strike because she lunged and sunk her blade into her assailant. Nearby, she saw Meliore shoot a bolt into another and sprint a few steps toward her. She brandished her crossbow and smashed it against another attacker. On the other side of Corbella, the friar stepped forward and struck out with a spear.

"WE THOUGHT YOU WERE DONE FOR!" he said with a grin. *"THOSE WERE SOME GOOD MOVES."*

Corbella went to say thanks but was immediately interrupted by another attack. They seemed to be coming without end. Her arms began to ache terribly and the weight of the blade dragged at her muscles. All at once, she saw a figure, decayed and disgusting dodge this way and that. He dove in, thrusting his blade at her and she was too fatigued to react. The whole world shuddered for a moment and she found her legs crumpling underneath her. It was as though her limbs had suddenly turned to jelly. She saw Meliore look at her in complete fright and bring her crossbow smashing down on the assailant's head. It was then that Corbella noticed his hand was clutching a dagger that was withdrawing from her chest. It looked bloody.

A sudden rush of warmth and unbelievable pain hammered her chest all in one moment and she collapsed on the ground, dropping her sword and clutching her chest. She saw blood on her hand when she removed it and stared at it in shock.

So this is how it ends? After everything, all our great escapes and near captures, there's no escape anymore?

Corbella chuckled as the pain subsided and a dizzying numbness came over her.

I guess I can't escape getting caught at some point.

She felt some hands picking her up and the boy pushing on her wound. The pain momentarily went away and her mind cleared a little from it. Meliore was crying above her, fighting with her crossbow and Friar Bartal was next to her, swinging his spear from side to side. She craned her head back. Alexandra and a group of the remaining knights were fighting like mad at their backs. She looked to where Corlieu and Axio Barbarossa had run off and caught a glimpse of them and a few knights fighting Axio Talphon. The flurry of their weapons was tremendous.

An odd thing then happened. The fighting around them slowed a moment and all heads turned in one direction. Corbella fought the pain and got up on her elbows. There were torches coming up the mountain slopes and many more coming along the mountainside. Alexandra gave a great cheer and the Prince yelled so loudly that Corbella thought her ear had ruptured. A group of horsemen wearing strange emblems came charging around the group, sweeping many of the attackers away.

"Meliore, what is this?" she managed to sputter out.

"WE'RE SAVED!" Meliore said gleefully, observing the battle raging around them. *"At least for the moment."*

When Meliore turned and looked down at Corbella her face grew pale. The Prince jumped up and went running out to a rider who stopped and saluted him. When the Prince came back, he conferred with Bartal and knelt down next to Corbella.

"THE PRINCE SAID HE SENT FOR SOMEONE TO TAKE CARE OF THAT WOUND," Bartal shouted. He knelt down as well and looked over her.

"Sorry," he said. "This is going to hurt a moment."

Corbella felt him tentatively examine the wound. Her eyes went wide and she gasped in pain.

"Is she okay?" asked Meliore nervously.

"I'm fine so far," said Corbella irritably. "I'm still alive you know."

"That wasn't…" Meliore responded quickly. "I mean, you know what I was getting at."

"If she slipped into a sleep, then I would be worried. It looks like the strike did not hit anything important however, so she'll be just fine," Bartal said.

A group of men adorned in robes arrived swinging bags off their backs. They saluted the Prince, who spoke to them rapidly. Bartal spoke to them as well and one of the men pulled out a flask and held it to Corbella's lips.

"Drink," said Bartal. "This is a type of Persian wine which will take away a lot of the pain."

Corbella guzzled away so earnestly that the man pulled the flask away, looking a little bewildered. The others went to work on her wound. Corbella decided not to look, and when she opened her eyes they were speaking to the Prince and Bartal, who smiled and nodded before the men hurried away.

"They said that you'll be just fine," said Bartal. "The blade missed any critical parts so you'll just have to give it some time. You're going to be very sore for a while and you might vomit from the amount of that wine you drank."

Corbella grimaced, unsure if it was her imagination or not but feeling as though her stomach was already protesting. She lay for a moment unthinkingly before sitting up in shock. She had forgotten that they were still in the midst of a battle.

"Where are the knights? And Alexandra? Has anyone seen Corlieu and Barbarossa?"

Meliore helped her to stand and Corbella winced as her wound protested. She bit back a cry of pain and looked around. The army that had come to their rescue was a sizable force, nearly on par with the army of Axio Talphon.

"THERE, LOOK!" cried Meliore, pointing off in the distance.

Corbella followed her finger and saw a flurry of shapes. It was Corlieu, a blond–haired man and Axio Barbarossa all fighting Talphon. How Talphon was able to fend off all three of them at once was a marvel to watch, and watch was all that they could do. Corbella knew she hadn't a hope of being able to help and she doubted there were many other warriors in the world who could match their fighting. The blond fighter swept in with a vicious strike, but Talphon was able to dodge it and sent him sprawling backwards with a kick. Corlieu came bounding up and struck down at his exposed leg, but Talphon merely twisted and rammed him out of the way with a double strike. Meliore gave a shriek when Corlieu crumpled down, but Alexandra was nearby and slowly helped him to his feet.

Only the two Axios remained in battle. Barbarossa and Talphon clashed weapon and shield. Strike by strike and moment by moment, they both fought without reserve. Every strike was potentially deadly and the force of their attacks was felt as shockwaves through the ground. One of Barbarossa's strokes went wide and was carried off by Talphon's blade. In an instant, however, Barbarossa dropped his shield and deflected Talphon's arm. The strike was halted and Barbarossa drove his down into Talphon's exposed side.

A piercing sound rose from the battlefield. A white light shone, blinding her for a moment before it faded. The noise remained however. It was so loud it seemed to echo against the clouds, but it passed up into the higher circles of the sky. There it vanished, into the vastness beyond the wide reaches of the world.

Chapter 23

Corlieu, Axio Barbarossa, Alexandra and the blond warrior slowly went back up the mountainside, flanked by a handful of Axio Barbarossa's remaining knights. The torches there had been relit, displaying the splendor of a great bonfire.

Alexandra broke the silence by turning to the young blond warrior.

Who…are you? I can see, an Order member that is to be sure, but who exactly?"

The warrior, slightly taken aback at her forwardness smiled.

"I am Captain Kaylee of the Empire of Nicaea. It is the Emperor's son, the Prince of Nicaea, who is being kept in your care.

"That he is," said Corlieu. "We learned this from Friar Bartal, who speaks his language. But how did you know he was with our party?"

"I was not certain initially," Kaylee explained. "But I rode up nearly to the army and obtained a blade, which I showed my Emperor. It was of the same make as that of the army that laid waste through our homelands, and since our Prince was missing, I thought he must be close."

"We thank you for your help in defeating Talphon, Captain," said Corlieu. "And rest assured that the Prince of Nicaea will be safely returned to you."

"We are in debt to you Corlieu," said Kaylee with a , turning to Barbarossa. "And that light, I have never seen anything like that. What was it? I thought I heard it speak to you!"

"It did," said Barbarossa. His hands were clasped behind his back and his brow furrowed. "It was Talphon's spirit. After I struck him down, something fled into the sky and the Talphon we knew appeared before me."

"And that scream!" said Corlieu. "I caught a glimpse of it as it shot away. It looked like a cloud."

"I cannot tell you what that was," said Barbarossa worryingly. "I felt it pass through me first and my mind went blank for the moment. It was then that the spirit appeared and greeted me before it fled into the sky."

The four of them continued through Barbarossa's sanctuary. It echoed with the sounds of grinding stone as the remaining knights took their places and solidified with arms up, holding their axes aloft once again. All at once, they were alone and standing by the door to Barbarossa's chamber.

"I have been puzzling over what might have led Axio Talphon on this path," Barbarossa said before stepping inside. "He didn't know what happened to him, his memory was too far lost to be able to tell of what befell him. He described it as a plague of the mind that took over both limbs and reason. Over time, his power as an Axio began to infect the lands and covered the populace in a sickness. The Arger of his sanctuary must have been the first to go. From there, they were reanimated and it was simply a matter of spreading out. Every enemy they killed or infected with that disease only increased their ranks."

"I recognized the Arger," said Alexandra. "In the battle, that filth still wore the emblem of an Axio's sanctuary. We fought and after dealing the killing blow, I took it from him."

She held it out for Barbarossa. It was a three–pointed star with a two–headed eagle on it. He turned it over and found a large cut running across the back.

"Yes," said Barbarossa, "this is his symbol. It was the head of Talphon's sanctuary you slew. Talphon must have been corrupted while he was in his sanctuary and in turn corrupted his Arger and the other keepers."

Barbarossa handed the emblem back to Alexandra and they all grew silent.

"Why did he go after our young Prince of Nicaea?" asked Kaylee. "The Prince knew nothing of our order."

"That's quite correct," said Barbarossa. "Perhaps as Talphon was looking for larger armies and sought to ally with the Nicaeans."

"We have been fighting against invaders from the south and east for ages now," said Kaylee. "Perhaps he thought that it would be easy to spread this corruption into our army as allies and needed something to grab onto to spread it, be it logic or loyalty."

"That might very well be the case," said Barbarossa. "It would explain the importance of the Prince. Aside from his royal birth, there's nothing of note that he could have offered at his age to the army."

They all drew silent and Corlieu bowed his head in thought.

It does make some sense. I never truly expected that a treasure or riches were being held in the besieged castle. Still, I never expected it to be a Prince held for ransom that was drawing Talphon and the army here.

"Is this over then?" asked Corlieu.

"It seems to be so," said Barbarossa, "the entire land is saved from this corruption, though many lives have been lost. The worst of this is over, for now."

Barbarossa stared off in the distance for a full minute before turning his gaze upon the others.

"I certainly hope it is not to be, but my heart tells me that before the next time you two lay down for another few centuries of sleep, I will be needed and we four will meet again."

No one spoke as Barbarossa stepped inside and the door slid shut. Corlieu felt his throat tighten and looked at Kaylee and Alexandra.

Then, as if on cue, they all turned and walked back down the hallway.

*****

Meliore helped Corbella up and they made their way to a rocky outcropping of the mountain. Friar Bartal had come to check on them a few moments prior and recommended a spot some ways off. He also gave them a great serving of food to enjoy.

"Courtesy of the Emperor of Nicaea," he said with a smile. "He's been ever so grateful to have his son back."

This was how Corbella and Meliore found themselves the day after the battle, dozing lazily against an amazingly warm rock and enjoying their meal. Back in Genoa, it would have been considered a moderate feast. The uncouth way it was presented would have only been balanced out by the sheer exoticness of it.

"You know," said Meliore. "This really hasn't been the bad life since we ran away."

"Speak for yourself. You haven't been stabbed!" Corbella replied.

""Ah you forget already," said Meliorie pointing to her side. "It still hurt when you were running around all CLANKETH CLANKETH like all sanity left your head. Still though, you are alive, the battle is over, the Prince of Nicaea has been returned, the Emperor is pleased, and we're sitting here with our bellies full in the warm sun. What could go wrong now?""

Corbella started to respond when the sound of breaking branches interrupted her.

"FINALLY, WE'VE GOT YOU!" came a shout.

She jumped and spun, glancing past Meliorie who shook in a startled jerk at the sudden uproar. She recognized the shape riding a horse towards them through the trees. As she stared, she saw it perk its ears and nicker. It was her horse, Mercurie.

"ALESSANDRO!" Meliore said, indignantly turning around and facing him. "I can't believe you followed us, things must really be slow if you had time to drag your nose all the way here."

"SHUT IT!" he yelled, pounding his legs so hard that Mercurie hopped.

He goaded the horse forward until he was only a length or two away from her. Behind him, the bushes separated and a small host of guards came out. They all were lightly armed and equipped mainly for speed. However, as they dismounted and approached the girls, they brought forth their lances and held them at the ready. Alessandro held out a hand against them.

"That won't be needed, their game is up and they'll surely see reason without the use of force. Now come, Meliore. It's a long way home and I'm eager to see what Father has in store for you."

Meliore was so astonished at his brashness that she found herself unable to say anything. How on earth did this buffoon and his henchmen manage to sneak their way past the Emperor's army unnoticed? Did they seriously believe they would be able to take them away unchallenged?

"How dare you, you slovenly fool," Corbella shouted back at him in the middle of a pained laugh. "We haven't fought our way through castles, armies and death to give in to the pathetic likes of you, and get off my horse!"

"Typical Corbella," sneered Alessandro. "This horse belongs to the family, not you. You were always so sharp with your words and grandiose with your stories but this time there is nobody to protect you and nowhere to run."

"Who's running?" she said, getting up gingerly and taking a step toward him.

"What happened to you anyways, did you trip and fall on a stick?" he asked, pointing to her wound.

"I think it's about time you leave," said Meliore. She had recovered enough from the shock of finding her brother all the way out here and walked confidently up to him. "We are not going back and there is no way you and this gaggle can make us," she said, hoisting up her crossbow.

Whatever it was in her tone must have struck a sore nerve with Alessandro, Meliore thought, for as she finished, he took a great arcing slash at her with the blunt end of his lance. She heard the whistle of wind and a cry from Corbella as the lance met her crossbow with a solid crack.

Meliore felt the tremor of the impact run down her arm. Her brother was fearsomely strong and her wrist tingled with the impact of the block. Still, she was determined and his words had lit the fire of defiance within her. She was not the same girl she was when they grew up, cowering and nervous, always trying to hide behind someone else and not knowing what to do. She was warrior now and had the wounds and determination to prove it.

"Don't make me hurt you," Alessandro said, pressing his weight forward until he was sparsely a few inches away.

"You can't," she said, breaking into a grin just before rocking back and planting her forehead forcefully against his nose.

Alessandro dropped his lance and cried out in pain. A fountain of blood erupted from his nose and he stepped backwards, collapsing on the ground and withering in pain. Behind him, however, the guards stepped forward with their lances drawn pressed down on the girls.

"Surrounded again…" said Meliore, holding her crossbow at the ready and backing up next to Corbella.

"…and against the odds," Corbella said with a laugh, drawing her sword. "But we've got each other and I'll be damned if anyone's going to take us back home so easily."

The guards charged and the girls took a step forward. Corbella cleaved through the row of lances with a steady strong slash in the same manner they had observed Corlieu fight. Meliore jumped back as one of the guards sought to drive his sword into her chest. She blocked it and slid her crossbow down the sword's blade until it crashed against the startled guard's face. He crumpled backwards without a word, but another guard came barreling in with his weapon raised over his head. She ducked down and felt something being flung over her.

It was a net. Unable to get back to feet, Meliore struggled and slashed, but the weight of it disabled her. Her crossbow was stuck and she was unable to untangle herself. She saw through the mesh that Corbella was stuck beside her.

"You two will *PAY FOR THIS DEARLY!*" yelled Alessandro from afar. His face was striped red with blood and his nose looked broken. "I see we're going to have to disable you somehow for the trip home so we can rest a little more easily at night." He rummaged in his side pocket, dropping a few things and finally pulling out a vial.

"I managed to purchase this at the Genoan dockside before I left. It's designed to make the consumer weak, feverish and suffering from stomach convulsions. I have enough for the trip home and you will find your hostility severely tempered by this."

Alessandro was laughing so deeply that he failed to notice a long stick inching its way downward from the trees. It hit the vial that Alessandro was holding before him and flew squarely in his mouth. Alessandro's eyes went wide and he looked stricken, doubling over to his hands and knees in a fit of coughing.

"CORLIEU!" Meliore cried just as he jumped down from the branch, from where he had been hanging upside down, and swung the stick.

Corlieu put a foot on Alessandro, kicking him over to face him. All around, Nicaean guards emerged from the woods, sabers drawn and grim determination on their faces.

"Who," stammered Alessandro, turning purple as Corlieu held him down with the weight of his foot. "Who are you?"

"Don't worry about that," Corlieu said. "Nobody you deserve to know."

The Nicaean guards separated and the Emperor emerged, looking around and whispering to his herald. The man yelled something at some of the guards and Meliore found hands pulling the netting off of her and helping her to her feet. One of the men held up her sword and she took it, her legs aching terribly from the blow. Corbella too was standing, a trail of blood coming down her arm from the reopened wound on her chest. Already, one of the

Nicaeans was at work on it.

"Who are you who break into this place, disturb my encampment and attack these girls?" asked the herald.

"I'm her brother, I was sent here to bring her home," squealed Alessandro, gasping for air underneath Corlieu's foot.

The Emperor motioned to his herald and spoke to him before sitting back.

"Did you send for them? Did you want to go home?" the herald asked the girls.

"Not in this lifetime," said Meliore while Corbella simply nodded.

"And that answer displeased him I'm guessing?" the herald continued. "So he and this band of ruffians tried to take you by force?"

Corlieu reached down and pulled out the vial from Alessandro's pocket. He tossed it to one of the guards, who brought it up to the Emperor. The Emperor's face twisted up in fury. For the first time, he spoke out loud.

"Not only were you going to take these girls by force, but you were going to poison them as well?" the Emperor said. "I know this poison well. The thieves and assassins that have tried to invade my land use a more concentrated form."

The Emperor calmed himself down upon glancing at the shocked look from the assembled people and then motioned to his herald again. The herald moved back a couple of inches as though to protect his ears before the Emperor stood up and spoke, his mercy non–existent.

"This action is incorrigible and I will make sure that you will pay. *GUARDS!*" he ordered. *"BIND THESE MEN TIGHTLY AND TAKE THEM WITH US! THEY SHALL CLEAN HORSE STALLS UNTIL THEY EXPIRE!"*

Alessandro cried out as the Nicaean guards took him and stared at Meliore, dumbfounded. His eyes were wide, unable to believe what just happened and for the first time in her life, scared of her.

As the Nicaeans began taking Alessandro's host away, Corbella jumped up and ran towards them.

"Wait!" she yelled.

They all looked at her in astonishment. Meliore saw Alessandro turn in surprise and hope. His face fell however when she pushed through them all and took hold of Mercurie.

"This horse is mine!" she said, leading him back to her cousin and throwing her arms around his neck as tears streamed down her face. "I thought I'd never see you again boy!"

Friar Bartal came up to the girls, he looked overjoyed. He flailed his arms and smacked Meliore across the back in absolute glee.

"What did I tell you Corlieu, these girls are something aren't they?"

"Corlieu," said Corbella, tying up Mercurie and walking up to him briskly until she was inches from his face. "What were you doing up there? Couldn't you have helped us beforehand? Were you…watching the whole thing?"

He and Bartal laughed and looked at them in amusement.

"We both were watching you," Corlieu said. "I wanted to see what would happen and up until the nets came out, it didn't look like you needed us at all."

"You two were great, swinging, fighting and whacking them all down," said the friar as he mimed the fight. "Nets are a dirty trick anyways. It's almost impossible to get out of those things."

"WE COULD HAVE GOTTEN SERIOUSLY HURT!" yelled both girls.

"Aware of that as I was, there is no better way to help someone other than to let them face things on their own and let them find out they can fight back."

Meliore didn't know what to say. She felt both accomplished at having fought Alessandro and his riders so well, and irritated that everyone seemed to have been watching them make a spectacle of themselves.

"Friar Bartal," said Corbella irritably. "Bring me that man with the Persian wine! My shoulder is killing me."

Chapter 24

The next week that passed was one of the best that the girls had ever known. The Emperor of Nicaea was so overjoyed at having his son back and so enthralled by the stories of their adventures that he orchestrated magnificent feasts and made them his guests of honor. The highlight of the first night was when she was waited on by a sulky looking Alessandro, occasionally prodded into serving Corbella and her dishes by an intense looking guard with a sword in his back.

Meliore was intrigued by the Nicaeans and tried to converse with them throughout that first evening. None of them understood her however and she gradually stopped until the second evening when Corlieu introduced Corbella and her to Captain Kaylee. Though a Nicaean, he understood them perfectly and was able to explain the festivities to them and a curious Alexandra.

Aside from when Kaylee had to attend to duties, the four of them found themselves riding and exploring the countryside. Alexandra was able to use a spare horse so they could all ride solo, and most of the daylight found them jumping and galloping around the foot of the mountain.

Dusk on the last night of the celebration found the four of them walking their horses back to the encampment.

"What are you two going to do?" asked Kaylee, breaking a long silence between them.

"What?" asked Meliore, not sure who the question was directed at and finding Kaylee looking at her.

"Now that the battle is over, the enemy has been driven away and everything looks pleasant again, what do you two hope to do?"

"I really don't know," said Meliore. "I suppose I haven't thought about it, I never expected to survive I think," she said and burst out laughing. "Do you have any ideas Corbella?"

"Not a clue in the wide world," said Corbella shaking her head. "This adventuring kind of life was a lot more harrowing than I ever would have thought. There's something about this peaceful life right now that just cannot be contended by anything else."

"You know," said Meliore leaning over, "you could always go back and marry that prince. I'm sure he'd take you back and you could live like that forever!"

"You, too, my dear cousin. You, too!" Corbella retorted.

Meliore grew red, recognizing her embarrassment. Earlier that day, both Kaylee and Alexandra asked them for a full account on how they came to the mountain. Meliore started the tale with the wedding, since it seemed most appropriate and had to endure Corbella's accusatory stares and uncomfortable squirming as Kaylee and Alexandra roared in laughter.

As they laughed again, Corbella squeezed her leg and Mercurie leapt into a canter with a snort. Meliore followed alongside her after a moment, throwing off her hat and helmet and letting the wind caress her long hair.

"ENJOY THE FREE AIR AND FRESH WIND, YOU THREE DEVILS!" yelled Kaylee. *"IT WON'T LAST FOREVER, BUT IT IS THE VICTORIOUS MOMENTS LIKE THESE THAT LIFE IS ALL ABOUT!"*

"May the heavens strike me down, but he's right," thought Meliore, looking at the others: Corbella with eyes closed and standing up off her seat, Alexandra not holding onto reigns and riding with her arms spread out like a bird, Kaylee with both fists in the air and a look of triumph on his face.

For the first real time in her life, Meliore felt accomplished. This is where she was meant to be and she was glad she endured the hard road and made it here. She yelled in excitement and held her arms out like Alexandra and let the wind and sun fill her spirit.

When they returned to their encampment, Friar Bartal broke the news that he was accepting an invitation from the Emperor to study with his scholars. He would learn as much as he could about the language of Hellas, both modern and ancient.

"My dear friends," said Bartal. "We have known each other a short while but you two are the most remarkable of all the people I have ever met. You have overcome deficiency and unfortunate circumstance to find yourselves now as veteran warriors, knights of Nicaea, and a whole host of other honorary things I lack the elegance and memory to describe appropriately."

"I…" began Corbella.

"Parting is such a sorrow, is it not?" said Bartal with a smile. "We'll meet again at some point. Trust me, in this life or in whatever comes afterwards, we will see each other. So go forth and do great things so you have many stories to tell when alas we do! I won't have any, it is a boring life in study and will need your entertainment."

Corbella laughed despite her tears and she and Meliore gave him a hug before he got atop his horse and began riding away. Meliore was about to turn when a blond figure came over and punched her in the shoulder.

"Forgot about me, did you two?" said Kaylee. "What for the heavens would a goodbye be without some bruising to remember us all by?"

"Kaylee!" shouted Meliore. "We thought you already left! I thought scouts were supposed to go first?"

"Ah dear, this is the great thing about being a Captain. I get to order the others to go ahead and get a chance to make my parting farewells," he said with a laugh. I have known you two for only a matter of a week but to me you are both sisters. Remember to fight hard and against all foes! Especially you, Corbella. You will need to in case Meliore gets caught unawares again!"

"Why you!" shouted Meliore. "Mind yourself or another Axio might put a foot in your gut again!"

Kaylee wrinkled his nose at her and went to say something before a look of shock came over his face and he turned this way and that.

"I had someone here who wanted a word with you. *BARTAL, WHERE IS THE PRINCE!*" he yelled.

Meliore turned around and saw the small, thin figure approaching them. It was the boy, the Prince of Nicaea.

"Thank you for freeing me from the castle," he said with only a few traces of an accent. "I am sorry I was of no help at first but I hope that everything that has happened since has sufficed."

Corbella laughed a moment and threw an arm around him.

"You helped save my life. If anything I am indebted to you. You are a true treasure!"

"*Corbella,*" whispered Meliore. "*I don't think that's a proper way to treat a prince.*"

"Oh, yes you're right," she said straightening up. "" said Corbella.

"No harm," said the Prince, bowing slightly to the girls and jumping behind Kaylee.

"Farewell!" said Kaylee and Bartal, turning and riding their horses off after the host.

Corlieu and Alexandra were nearby and had also been saying their goodbyes. Now the four of them stood, watching the dust of the army rise up into the sky. Corbella remained there until the final clouds of dust settled and the land around them was quiet. The sounds of birds overtook the air and the tremor of earth under feet and hooves slowly became still.

"In all seriousness, what are we going to do now?" Meliore asked out loud.

"I know not about you three," said Alexandra, "but I have to remain here to guard and upkeep the sanctuary of Axio Barbarossa. You all are welcomed to stay a few days more until you have made plans."

"I suppose there's no way we all could remain there," asked Meliore halfheartedly.

"And live off of the sanctuary?" said Alexandra in mock contempt. "Please, this is not a royal lounge. Don't make me throw you two out!"

"There'll be no need for that," said Corlieu with a snicker. He turned to Meliore and Corbella.

"I have some ideas if it is easy living you're after. Now that my mission is done it seems, I have little left to do until the next time I need to sleep."

"When will that be?" asked Corbella in a suddenly nervous tone.

"Oh...perhaps about another fifty or sixty years at least," said Corlieu. "Never have I been awaken prematurely. I am thankful that the spontaneous sleeping has ceased, but still, all the effects are not known to me yet."

"Fifty or sixty years…" muttered Corbella. She looked askance at Meliore. "Do you think we should go off with Corlieu, at least until we can get enough wealth to live off on our own?"

"Without a doubt, so long as we three don't go ripping off any poor unfortunate girls," Meliore said, casting a menacing look at Corlieu.

"You have my sincerest affirmation that I won't be doing that again. I cannot afford two more leeches and another plight such as the one you two put me through!" he said to an uproar of laugher and a barrage of kicks.

"Now," said Meliore. "What is there to eat? Anything at all but, lest I lose my mind, don't show me another…"

"…biscuit?" interjected Corbella, holding one up out of her bag.

"Don't you ever run out of those?" said Meliore with a repulsive expression. "They're probably all rotten by now anyways."

"Meliore," said Corlieu clapping her on the shoulder. "Wherever you go, there'll always be biscuits to be had."

"Lovely, just lovely," she said.

"But fortunately, I have some better food at the sanctuary," said Alexandra.

"Let's be off then!" the three of them said, following her into the side of the mountain.

The End.

The Renegades of Genoa